Sylvia

Also by Leonard Michaels

Shuffle ◆ Autobiographical Fiction
The Men's Club ◆ A Novel
I Would Have Saved Them if I Could ◆ Stories
Going Places ◆ Stories
West of the West: Imagining California ◆ *Coeditor*
The State of the Language 1990 ◆ *Coeditor*
The State of the Language 1980 ◆ *Coeditor*

Sylvia

A FICTIONAL MEMOIR

Illustrations by
Sylvia Bloch

MICHA

LEONARD
MICHAELS

MERCURY HOUSE
San Francisco

Copyright © 1990, 1992 by Leonard Michaels

P.B. 134

Published by Mercury House, San Francisco, California.
A portion of this work was previously published in *Shuffle,* 1990,
Farrar, Straus & Giroux, and is reprinted by arrangement.
Distributed to the trade by Consortium Book Sales & Distribution

United States Constitution, First Amendment: Congress shall make no
law respecting an establishment of religion, or prohibiting the free
exercise thereof; or abridging the freedom of speech, or of the press;
or the right of the people peaceably to assemble, and to petition the
Government for a redress of grievances.

Mercury House and colophon are registered trademarks of
Mercury House, Incorporated.

Epigraph by Adam Zagajewski from "Fruit," included in *Canvas*
(Farrar, Straus & Giroux, 1992).

Manufactured in the United States of America

Library of Congress Cataloging-in-Publication Data
Michaels, Leonard, 1933-
    Sylvia / Leonard Michaels. ... 1st ed.
        p. cm.
    ISBN 1-56279-029-3 : $10.00
        1. Title.   92-16541
PS3563.I273S95   1992   CIP
813'.54—DC20
10   9   8   7   6   5   4   3   2   1

*How unattainable life is, it only reveals
its features in memory
in nonexistence.*

—Adam Zagajewski

Sylvia

I N 1 9 6 0, after two years of graduate school at Berkeley, I returned to New York without a Ph.D. or any idea what I'd do, only a desire to write stories. I'd also been to graduate school at the University of Michigan, from 1953 to 1956. All in all, five years of classes in literature. I don't know how else I might have spent those five years, but I didn't want to hear more lectures, study for more exams, or see myself growing old in the library. There was an advertisement in the school paper for someone to take a car from Berkeley to New York, expenses paid. I made a phone call. A few days later, I was driving a Cadillac convertible through mountains and prairies, going back home, an over-specialized man, twenty-seven years old, who smoked cigarettes and could give no better account of himself than to say "I love to read." It doesn't qualify the essential picture, but I had a lot of friends, got along with my parents, and women liked me. Speeding toward the great city in a big, smooth-flowing car that wasn't mine, I felt humored by the world.

My parents' apartment on the Lower East Side of Manhattan, four rooms and a balcony, was too small for another adult, but I wouldn't be staying long. Anyhow, my mother let me feel like a child. It seemed natural. "What are you doing?" she said.

"Washing dishes? Please, please, go away. Sit down. Have a cup of coffee."

My father sighed, shook his head, lit a cigar. Saying nothing, he told me that I hadn't done much to make him happy.

From their balcony, fourteen stories high, I looked down into Seward Park. Women sat along the benches, chatting. Their children played in the sandbox. Basketball and stickball games, on courts nearby, were in process morning and afternoon. On Sundays, a flea market would be rapidly set up in a corner of the park—cheap, bright, ugly clothing strewn along the benches. In the bushes, you could talk to a man about hot cameras and TV sets. At night, beneath the lush canopy of sycamores and oaks, prostitutes brought customers. Beyond the park, looking north, I saw Delancey Street, the mouth of the Williamsburg Bridge eating and disgorging traffic. Further north were the Empire State Building and the Chrysler Building. Ever since I was a little kid, I'd thought of them as two very important city people. A few degrees to the right, I saw the complicated steel-work of the 59th Street Bridge. To the west, beyond Chinatown (where Arlene Ng, age ten, my first great love, once lived) and beyond Little Italy (where they shot Joey Gallo in Umberto's Clam House on Mulberry Street), loomed Wall Street's financial buildings and the Manhattan Bridge. Trucks, cars, and trains flashed through the grid of cables, crossing the East River to and from Brooklyn. Freighters progressed slowly, as if in a dream, to and from the ocean. In the sky, squadrons of pigeons made grand loops, and soaring gulls made line drawings. There were also streaking sparrows, and airplanes heading toward India and Brazil. All day and night, from every direction, came the hum of the tremendum.

I talked for hours on the telephone, telling my friends that I was home, and I sat up late at the kitchen table, drinking coffee, reading, and smoking. Most of the city slept. In the quiet, I heard police sirens as far away as Houston Street. Sometimes, I was awakened around noon or later by the smells of my mother's cooking which, like sunlight, became more subtle as the hours passed. Days were much alike. I didn't know Monday from Wednesday until I saw it in the newspaper. I'd forget immediately. After my parents had gone to bed, I'd step out to buy *The Times*, then stare at the columns of want ads. Among thousands upon thousands of jobs, none said my name. I wanted to do something. I didn't want something to do. Across the darkened living room, down the hall, in the big bed with my mother, my father lay snoring.

Whatever my regrets about school—lost years, no Ph.D.—I wasn't yet damaged by judgment. I hadn't failed badly at anything—like Francis Gary Powers, for example, whose name I heard every day. His U-2 spy plane had been shot down over Russia, and he'd failed to kill himself before being captured. Instead, he confessed to being a spy. President Eisenhower, who claimed the U-2 was a weather plane, looked like a liar.

There were few heroes. Malcolm X and Fidel Castro, fantastically courageous, were figures of violent disorder. They had both been in jail. But even in sports, where heroes are simple, they could be the focus of violence. A mob swarmed out of the stands after a ballgame, surrounded the great Mickey Mantle, tore off his hat, clawed his face, and punched him in the jaw so hard they had to take X rays to see if the bone was broken.

The odor of fresh newsprint, an oily film on my fingertips, mixed with cigarette smoke and the taste of coffee. Pages turned and crackled like fire, or like breaking bones. I read that 367 were killed in traffic accidents during the Memorial Day weekend, and, since the first automobile, over a million had been killed on our roads, more than in all our wars. And look: Two sisters were found dead in their apartment on Gracie Square, in the bathtub, wearing nightgowns. A razor lay in the hand of one of the sisters. Blood wasn't mentioned. This was old-style journalism, respectfully distanced from personal tragedy. Nothing was said about how the sisters had arranged themselves in the tub. Their life drained away as the crowd vomited out of the stands to worship and mutilate Mickey Mantle. There were really no large meanings, only cries of the phenomena. I read assiduously. I kept in touch with my species.

About a week after I arrived, I phoned Naomi Kane, a good pal from the University of Michigan. We'd spent many hours together drinking coffee in the Student Union, center of romantic social life, gossip, and general sloth. Naomi, who had grown up in Detroit, in a big, comfortable house with elm trees all

around, lived now in Greenwich Village, on the sixth floor of an old brick tenement on MacDougal Street.

"Push the street door hard," she said. "There is no bell and the lock doesn't work."

From my parents' apartment I walked to the subway, caught the F train, took a seat, and was stunned into insentient passivity. The train shrieked through the rock bowels of Manhattan to the West Fourth Street station. I walked up three flights of stairs in the dingy, resonant cavern, then out into the light of a hot Sunday afternoon.

Village streets carried slow, turgid crowds of sightseers, especially MacDougal Street, the main drag between Eighth and Bleecker, the famous Eighth Street Bookshop at one end, the famous San Remo bar at the other. I'd walked MacDougal Street innumerable times during my high school days, when my girlfriend lived in the Village, and, later, all through college, when my second girlfriend lived in the Village. But I'd been gone two years. I hadn't seen these huge new crowds, and new stores and coffeehouses all along the way. I hadn't sensed the new apocalyptic atmosphere.

Around then, Elvis Presley and Allen Ginsberg were kings of feeling, and the word *love* was like a proclamation with the force of *kill*. The movie *Hiroshima, mon amour*, about a woman in love with death, was a big hit. So was *Black Orpheus*, where death is in loving pursuit of a woman. I noticed a graffito chalked on the wall of the West Fourth Street subway station: FUCK HATE. Another read: Mayor Wagner is a lesbian. Wonderfully stupid,

I thought, but then the sense came to me. I remembered a newspaper photo showing the city's first meter maids, a hundred strong, in slate blue uniforms. They stood in lines, in a military manner, as Mayor Wagner reviewed them. Ergo: a lesbian. Before 1960, could you have had this thought, made this joke? There had been developments in sensibility, a visionary contagion derived maybe from drugs—marijuana, heroin, uppers, downers—the poetry of common conversation. Weird delirium was in the air, and in the sluggish, sensual bodies trudging down MacDougal Street. I pressed among them until I came to the narrow, sooty-faced tenement where Naomi lived.

I pushed in through the door, into a long hallway painted with greenish enamel, giving the walls a fishy sheen. The hall went straight back through the building to the door of a coffee-house called The Fat Black Pussy Cat. Urged by the oppressive, sickening green walls, hardly a foot from either shoulder, I walked quickly. Just before the door to The Fat Black Pussy Cat, I came to a stairway with an ironwork banister. I climbed up six flights through the life of the building. A phonograph played blues; an old lady screamed in Italian at a little boy named Bassano; a hall toilet was clattering and flushing, flushing, flushing. At the sixth floor, I turned right and walked down a dark hallway, narrower than the one at street level. No overhead lights burned beyond the landing. There was the glow of a window at the end of the hallway. Brittle waves of old linoleum cracked like eggshells beneath my steps. Naomi's door, formerly the entrance to an office, had a clouded glass window. I knocked.

She opened. With a great hug, she welcomed me into a small kitchen.

Behind her, I saw a refrigerator and stove. A half-wall partition separated the kitchen from the living room, with a gap that let you pass through. The partition served as a shelf for a telephone, papers, books, and pieces of clothing. A raw brick wall dominated the living room. The floor was wide, rough, splintery planks, as in a warehouse. It was strewn with underwear, shoes, and newspapers. Light, falling through a tall window, came from the west. The window looked over rooftops all the way to the Hudson River, then beyond to the cliffs of New Jersey. Another tall window, in the kitchen, looked east across Mac-Dougal Street at a tenement just like this one. I supposed that Naomi's apartment, in the middle of Greenwich Village, must be considered desirable. Naomi said, "Don't make wisecracks. The rent is forty bucks a month." Then she introduced me to Sylvia Bloch.

She stood barefoot in the kitchen dragging a hairbrush down through her long, black, wet Asian hair. Minutes ago, apparently, she had stepped out of the shower, which was a high metal stall in the kitchen, set on a platform beside the sink. A plastic curtain kept water from splashing onto the kitchen floor. She said hello but didn't look at me. Too much engaged, tipping her head right and left, tossing the heavy black weight of hair like a shining sash. The brush swept down and ripped free until, abruptly, she quit brushing, stepped into the living room, dropped onto the couch, leaned back against the brick wall, and went totally limp. Then, from behind long black bangs, her eyes moved, looked at me. The question of what to do with my life was resolved for the next four years.

Sylvia was slender and suntanned. Her hair fell below the middle of her back. Long bangs obscured her eyes, making her look shy or modestly hiding, and also shorter than average. She was five-six. Her eyes, black as her hair, were quick and brilliant. She had a high fine neck, wide shoulders, narrow hips, delicately shaped wrists and ankles. Her figure and the smooth length of her face, with its wide sensuous mouth, reminded me of Egyptian statuary. She wore a weightless cotton Indian dress with an intricate flowery print. It was the same brown hue as her skin.

We sat in the living room until Naomi's boyfriend arrived. He was black, tall, light complexioned. Mixed couples were common, especially with Jewish women, but I was surprised. Conversation was awkward for me, determined not to stare at Sylvia. The summer heat and the messy living room with its dirty floor destroyed concentration, discouraged talk. Things were said, but it was dull obligatory stuff. Mainly we perspired and looked at one another. After a while, Naomi suggested we go for a walk. I was relieved and grateful. We all got up and left the apartment and went down into the street, staying loosely together, heading toward Washington Square Park. Naomi came up beside me and whispered, "She's not beautiful, you know."

The remark embarrassed me. My feelings were too obvious. I'd been hypnotized by Sylvia's flashing exotic effect. Naomi sounded vaguely annoyed, as though I'd disappointed her. She wanted to talk, wanted to put me straight, but we weren't alone. I said "Ummm." Incapable of anything better, I was literally meaningless. Naomi then said, as if she were making a concession, "Well, she is very smart."

We were supposed to have dinner together and go to a movie, but Naomi and her boyfriend disappeared, abandoning Sylvia and me in the park. Neither of us was talking. We'd become social liabilities, too stupid with feeling to be fun. We continued together, as if dazed, drifting through dreamy heat. We'd met for the first time less than an hour ago, yet it seemed we'd been together, in the plenitude of this moment, forever. We walked for blocks without becoming flirtatious, barely glancing at each other, staying close. Eventually, we turned back toward the tenement; with no reason, no words, slowly turning back through the crowded streets, then into the dismal green hall and up six flights of stairs, and into the squalid apartment, like a couple doomed to a sacrificial assignation. It started without beginning. We made love until afternoon became twilight and twilight became black night.

Through the tall open window of the living room we saw the night sky and heard the people proceed along MacDougal Street, as in a lunatic carnival, screaming, breaking glass, wanting to hit, needing meanness. Someone played a guitar in a nearby apartment. Someone was crying. Lights flew across the walls and ceiling. The city made its statement in the living room. None of it had to do with us, lying naked on the couch, just wide enough for two, against the brick wall. Released by sex into simple confidence, we talked. Sylvia told me she was nineteen, and had recently left the University of Michigan, where she had met Naomi. Some years earlier, Sylvia's father, who worked for the Fuller Brush company, died of a heart attack. The doctors had told him not to smoke and he tried to give it up, tearing his cigarettes in half, carrying the halves behind his ears until he couldn't not put one between his lips and light it. Her mother was a housewife who did well playing the stock market as a hobby. Soon after her husband's death, she became ill with cancer. Sylvia visited her in the hospital every day after high school. She said her mother became exquisitely sensitive as she declined, until even the odor of the telephone cord beside her bed nauseated her. After her mother died, Sylvia lived with an aunt and uncle in Queens. She had bad dreams and heard jeering voices, as if the loss of her parents had made her contemptible. To get out of New York, she applied to the University of Michigan and Radcliffe. Her boyfriend was at Harvard. She described him as very kind and nice looking, a lean, fine-featured blond. She said she was brighter than her boyfriend, but Radcliffe turned her down. They didn't need her; they could easily fill every class with German Jews. Sylvia took the rejection personally. That was the end of her boyfriend. Her present boyfriend worked in a local restaurant. He was a tall, sweet, handsome Italian; very sensitive and loving. He would show up tonight, she said. His swimsuit was in the apartment and he'd come for it after work.

Sylvia was telling me how she'd met Naomi, and then telling me how much she loved Naomi. "But Naomi loves me in theory, not in practice," said Sylvia. "She's very critical, always complaining because she can't find a shoe or her glasses or something in the apartment. She sometimes threatens not to come home if I don't clean up."

"Really?"

I was listening without hearing.

The boyfriend would show up tonight. Sylvia hadn't mentioned a boyfriend before she let me take off her clothes. I felt deceived. I wanted to go. She had a boyfriend. I'd have done it anyway, maybe, but I felt suddenly distanced from Sylvia, as if I'd dropped through the darkness into a well, darkness more dense. I wanted to get out and I imagined my clothes on the floor beside the bed. I could reach down, grab my underwear and pants, dress, go. I didn't move.

"He has a key?"

"No."

"The door is locked?"

"Yes."

"Look, I should go. I'll phone you in the morning."

"Stay."

She got up. Without turning on a light, which would show in the glass window of the door, she moved quickly in the chaos of the apartment, shoving books and papers about, tossing pieces of clothing, and then she found it, with blind feel only, a rag amid rags. His swimsuit. She hung it on the doorknob outside the apartment by the jock, then returned to the bed.

We lay in the balmy darkness, waiting for him. I wanted to get dressed, but I didn't move. After a while we heard a slow trudge coming up the stairway. It was a man. He seemed to heave himself up from step to step, wearily. We heard him on the linoleum in the hallway. From the weight of his steps, I figured he knew Sylvia had been unfaithful. He was big. He could break my head. His steps ended at the door, ten feet from where we lay. He didn't knock. He'd seen his swimsuit and was contemplating it, reading its message. He'd worked all day, he'd climbed six flights of steps, and he was rewarded with this disgusting spectacle. I supposed he wasn't stupid, but even a genius might kick in the flimsy door, and make a moral scene. He said, "Sylvia?" His quizzical tone carried no righteousness, only the fatigue and pain of his day. We lay very still, hardly breathing, bodies without mass or contour, dissolving, becoming the darkness. From his tone, from his one word, "Sylvia," I read his mind, understood his anguish. She'd done painful things before. He didn't want to prove to himself that she was in the apartment. He'd go stomping away down the hall. He'd fly down the stairs. Never come back. His voice was there again.

"Sylvia?"

Then he did it, he went away, stomping down the hall, down the stairs. His voice stayed with me. I felt sorry for him, and responsible for his disappointment. Mainly, I was struck by Sylvia's efficiency, how speedily she'd exchanged one man for another. Would it happen to me, too? Of course it would, but she lay beside me now and the cruel uncertainty of love was only an idea, a moody flavor, a pleasing sorrow of the summer night. We turned to each other, renewed by the drama of betrayal, and made love again.

Afterwards, Sylvia sat naked on the window ledge, outlined against the western skyline of the city and the lights of New Jersey. She stared at me and seemed to collect a power of decision, or to wonder what decision had been made. What had we just done? What did it mean? Years later, in fury, she would say, "The first time we went to bed. The first time . . ." resurrecting the memory with bitterness, saying I'd made her do extreme things. She said nothing about her boyfriend, and remembered only the sex, the indulgences. I'd wanted too much. She'd given too much. Years later, I still owed her something. It couldn't be estimated, or even fully expressed. An infinite debt of feeling.

At dawn, having slept not one minute, we went down into the street. The shining residue of night was strewn along the curb and overflowing trash cans, beginning to stink in the early light and heat. Broken, heaving sidewalks, the crust of a discontented, restless earth, oozed moisture and a steamy glow. There was no traffic; no people. Between dark and day, the city stood in stunned, fetid slumber. It had been deeply used. On a bench, in a small grassy area set back from Sixth Avenue, we sat and stared into each other's eyes, adoring, yet with a degree of reserve, or belated concern to see who we'd been to bed with for the last ten hours.

Sylvia said she was leaving for summer school at Harvard the next day. Instantly, I thought of her former boyfriend. He would be there. I felt jealous. I had no claim on Sylvia's fidelity and perhaps I didn't want it, but I felt jealous. She'd said she liked his blond looks, his gentle and Gentile old-money manners.

I supposed, Sylvia being so dark, she found the blond irresistible. It wasn't over between them. He was in Cambridge; she wasn't—and that was all. They'd soon be together. She'd see him. Old sentiments would revive. I'd lose her. Then she asked if I would come up to Cambridge and live with her. She held her face high, stiff with anticipation, as if to receive a blow.

I see her. Maybe I know what I'm looking at.

I was taken by highlights along her cheekbones and the luscious expectancy in her lower lip. I liked the Asian cast of her face, its smoothness, length, and tilt of its bones. Her straight black hair, against a look of cool dark blood, seemed to bear on the question of me in Cambridge. I sensed that she expected to hear me say no, expected to be hurt. But the way she held herself was imperial. She had told me the story of her life, eliminated a boyfriend, and asked me to live with her. I don't remember saying yes or no.

There was much to think about. None of it had to do with how Sylvia's cheekbones caught the light, or the luscious weight of her lower lip, or the cool focus of her eyes. But I kept seeing her face. I didn't think. I also saw the swimsuit turned inside out, hanging by the jock, like the carcass of a chicken disemboweled.

A week later I took the train to Boston. Sylvia moved out of her dormitory. We found a room near the university in a big house with shadowy passages.

I took the train. We found a room . . .

The truth is I didn't know what I was doing exactly, or why I was in Cambridge. Sylvia wanted me to be there. I had no immediate practical reason to be elsewhere—no job, nothing to do. My desire to write stories was nothing to do. It wouldn't pay. It wasn't work. When I looked at Sylvia's face, I liked what I saw, but I still wasn't sure why I was in Cambridge. I was sure of little. I missed her during the week she was gone from New York, but my feelings were only as strong as they were uncertain. Being with her in Cambridge, I felt no urgency to be anywhere else. It would be a brilliant, blooming, fragrant summer. I had a girlfriend. No obligations. I had only to be.

The room was in a house full of heavy, stolid things with white sheets thrown over them. Blinds were drawn, doors shut, defending against light and air. A man in his sixties lived in the house, creeping amid masses and shadows. He used almost nothing, apparently, and kept things undisturbed, hidden, as if waiting for the true owner of the house to return and pull away the sheets, use the furniture, live here. It came to me that someone close to him had died, and the man's life had stopped, too, or he feared death extremely, and so brought about this eerily reduced condition, using less and less, changing nothing, moving only in the shadows. He wasn't guilty of being in this world. Since he didn't exist, he'd never die.

The room was on the second floor. It had gray floral wall-paper, a mahogany dresser, two lavishly upholstered chairs—all wood surfaces veneered in hard slick brown—and a giant bed that stood high off the floor. Sitting on the edge of the bed, Sylvia's feet dangled in the air. She looked like a child. Pulling back the bedcovers demanded a strong grip and snap. Sheets were tucked in tight, making a hard flat field, perfect for a corpse. The mattress, unusually thick, like a fat luxurious heart, was sealed, lashed down by bedcovers and sheets. Basically, an excellent bed, but resistant to the pressures of a living human shape. It was an excellent, principled bed with a hatred of comfort. We used it most of the night, high above the floor, to make love.

When we came down in the morning, the man sat waiting in a straight-backed chair in the parlor. He was bald, gaunt, lean as a plank. His long platter face stared at the floor between his knees, as if into a pool of trouble.

"You two will have to go," he said. The command was drawn from a strange personal hell of New England propriety and constipation. In the middle of the night, maybe, he heard us. It occurred to him that Sylvia and I were touching, doing evils to each other's body, though we labored to be quiet, and fucked with Tantric subtlety, measuring pleasure slow and slow, out of respect for his ethical domain. He'd begun thinking things, driving himself to this moral convulsion. We didn't ask why we had to go. It was clear and final. We had to do it—go. We went back up to our room, packed, made no fuss, and were soon adrift in the busy, hot, bright streets around Harvard Square, carrying our bags.

Sylvia refused to return to her dormitory, though we had no place to go if we stayed together. I couldn't reason with her, couldn't argue. As far as she was concerned, she had no dormitory room, no place but here in the street with me.

The glorious summer day made things more difficult. Storefronts and windshields flashed threats. Everyone walked with energetic purpose. They belonged in Cambridge and were correct. We'd been thrown into the street. For this to have happened, one must have done something wrong. We were embarrassed and confused, squinting in the sunlight, carrying bags, the weight of blighted romance. I expected to spend the night in a sleazy hotel or in a park, but then, after phoning friends, we heard about a house where three undergraduates lived, in a working-class neighborhood, a long walk from the university. Maybe they'd rent us a room. We didn't phone. We went there, just showed up with our bags.

It was an ugly falling-down sloppy happy house. One of the men began talking to Sylvia, the moment he saw her, in baby talk. She said, "Hello." He said, "Hewo," with a goofy grin. She thought he was hilarious, and she loved being treated like a little girl in a house full of men. They all treated her the same way, affectionately teasing. She inspired it: shy, hiding behind long bangs, darkly sensuous. There was one empty room in the house. Nobody said we couldn't have it.

In the mornings Sylvia went to class and I tried to begin writing stories. Our room, just off the kitchen, was noisy with refrigerator traffic and running water. Sometimes people stood outside the door talking. I didn't mind. After our night in the mausoleum, I liked noises. The soft suck and thud of a refrigerator door was good. The sound of talking was good.

Sylvia was gone during the day, in class or studying in a library on campus. At night there were some irascible moments, heavy sighs, angry whispers, but the room was narrow, hot, airless. There were mosquitoes. Nothing personal. Through most of the slow, lovely summer, we were happy. Sylvia was taking a class in art history. We went to museums, and worked together on her papers. I didn't write any stories that I didn't tear up and throw away. The writing was no good, but I liked being with Sylvia and this life in Cambridge.

One afternoon, sitting on the front steps, waiting for Sylvia to return from class, I spotted her far down the street, walking slowly. When she saw me looking at her, she walked more slowly. Her right sandal was flapping. The sole had torn loose. At last she came up to me and showed me how a nail had poked up through the sole. She had walked home on the nail, sole flapping, her foot sloshing in blood. What else could she do? She smiled wanly, suffering, but good-spirited.

I said she could have had the sandal fixed or walked barefoot or called for a taxi. There was something impatient in my voice. She seemed shocked. Her smile went from wan to screwy, perturbed, injured. I couldn't call back the impatience in my voice, couldn't undo its effect. For days thereafter, Sylvia walked about Cambridge pressing the ball of her foot onto the nail, bleeding. She refused to wear other shoes. I pleaded, I argued with her. Finally, she let me take the sandal to be repaired. I was grateful. She was not grateful. I was not forgiven.

"Go, I don't love you. I hate you. I don't hate, I despise you. If you love me, you'll go. I think we can be great friends and I'm sorry we never became friends."

"Can I get you something?"

"A menstrual pill. They're in my purse."

I found the little bottle and brought her a pill.

"Go now."

I lay down beside her. We slept in our clothes.

(Journal, December 1960)

At the end of the summer we returned to New York. Naomi moved out of the MacDougal Street apartment. Sylvia and I moved in. By then, fighting every day, we'd become ferociously intimate.

Like a kid having a tantrum, she would get caught up in the sound of her own screaming. Screaming because she was screaming, screaming, screaming, as if building a little chamber of rage, herself at the center. It was all hers. She was boss. I wasn't allowed inside. Her eyes and teeth were bright blacks and whites, everything exaggerated and contorted, like the maelstrom within. There was nothing erotic in this picture, and yet we sometimes went from fighting to sex. No passport was required. There wasn't even a border. Time was fractured, there was no cause and effect, and one thing didn't even lead toward another. As in a metaphor, one thing was another. Raging, hating, I wanted to fuck, and she did too.

Fights often began without warning. I'd be saying something ordinary and neutral, but Sylvia was suddenly rigid, staring at me. She knocked the telephone off the shelf. I stopped talking, startled, jerked to attention. She knocked the cup and saucer that had been sitting beside the telephone to the floor. They smashed to pieces. Now she was screaming, denouncing me, and I was screaming back at her. She went for the radio, to fling it against the wall, and I lunged at her, trying to stop her. She twisted loose and came at me. Then it was erotic; anyhow, sexual. Afterwards, usually, she slept. Neither of us mentioned what had happened. From yelling to fucking. From unreal to real was how it felt.

Ordinary or violent, the sex was frequent, exhausting more than satisfying. Sylvia said she'd never had an orgasm. As if I were the one who stood between her and that ultimate pleasure, she announced, "I will not live my whole life without an orgasm." She said she'd had several lovers better than I was. She wanted to talk about them, I think, make me suffer details.

I began trying to write again. Sylvia began taking classes at NYU, a few blocks away across Washington Square Park, to complete her undergraduate work. She asked me what she ought to declare as her major. I said if I were doing it over, I'd major in classics. I should have said nothing. She registered for Latin and Greek, ancient history, and a class in eighteenth-century English literature. She had to learn the complex grammars of two languages, read long poems and fat novels, and write papers, all while living in squalor and fighting with me every day. It seemed to me a maniacal program. I expected confusion and disaster, but she was abnormally bright and did well enough.

There was no desk in the apartment, but Sylvia didn't need such conveniences, didn't even seem to notice their absence. I don't think she ever complained about anything in the miserable apartment, not even about the roaches, only about me. She studied sitting on the edge of the bed in a mess of papers. Her expression would go flat, her body limp. She would be utterly still except for her eyes. She didn't scratch, didn't stretch. She was doing the job, getting it over with. I'd sit with her sometimes for hours, reading a novel or a magazine. We ate together in bed, usually noodles, frozen vegetables, and orange juice, or else we went out for pizza or Chinese food. Neither of us cooked. My mother often gave us food. I'd carry it back to MacDougal Street after our visits downtown, two or three times a month.

One night, after dinner at my parents' apartment, my mother slipped away to the bedroom with Sylvia's coat and sewed up a tear in the sleeve. As we were about to leave, she surprised Sylvia with the mended coat. Sylvia seemed grateful and affectionate. In the street, however, she became hysterical with indignation, saying she'd been humiliated. I tried to make her understand that my mother was being sweet, doing something good for Sylvia. My mother intended kindness, not a comment on Sylvia's coat. I didn't say that Sylvia made a pitiable, waiflike impression in the torn coat. I said my mother wanted Sylvia to like her. Saying such things, I embarrassed myself. Then I became angry. What difference did motives make? Sylvia wanted to be pitied; my mother wanted to be liked. Who could care? What mattered was that my mother's gesture had been affectionate. To defend her against Sylvia brought up questions of loyalty. Maybe that was the point. But, to my mind, my mother needed no defense. I was wrong to defend her. I shut up. Sylvia could interpret things however she liked. I couldn't instruct her in feeling, and I refused to sink into a poisonous and boring morass of motives.

Thereafter, I visited my parents alone.

Sometimes, as if I were visiting out of bitter determination rather than a simple desire to be with them, I sat at the table and ate like a solemn pig. You like to feed me? Good, that's why I'm here, I'm eating. In my own eyes, I seemed irrational, ill-tempered, spiteful, and unhappily confused about everything in my life. My mother had done too much for me, beginning when I was a little kid who never went two weeks without an ear infection or lung disease. She carried me through the streets to the doctor because I couldn't walk, always too sick, too weak.

She sat beside my bed all night lest I were kidnapped by death. It's hard to forgive self-sacrifice. As for Sylvia's sensitivity to imagined insult, that was pathological, not on the side of life. My mother's cooking was life.

"Who needs restaurants?" said my father, slurping his soup. "You can't find better food no place."

My mother sewed up the tear in the sleeve of Sylvia's coat. She didn't ask first. Big deal. She'd never do that again. I told her it was a mistake. I knew she would be shocked and her feelings would be hurt, but I had to tell her. I wanted to tell her. She didn't in the least understand. I tried to explain how a person might be annoyed if you make a fuss over her torn clothing. It is important not to notice such things. Her personal business, not yours. The more I talked, the more exasperated I felt. I raised my voice, as if I were criticizing her for doing what she believed was nice. What did I believe? I also believed it was nice. I was criticizing her for doing what I believed was nice.

Barely five feet tall and always cooking, cleaning, shopping, sewing. To criticize "the Mommy"—my father's expression— was, even if correct, incorrect in the eyes of God. It was close to evil. In the background with his cigar, watching television, brooding, he made gloomy, silent judgments. ("That's how you talk to the Mommy? What's the matter with you? Don't you know better?")

I rode the F train to West Fourth Street, then hurried through the garish carnival of MacDougal Street, where tourists came nightly from all over the city to sit in neighborhood coffee shops like Cafe Bizarre, Cafe Wha, Take Three, Cock and Bull, and Cafe Figaro, where they could listen to somebody strum a guitar and sing through his sinuses like a hillbilly. I entered our building and, without getting winded, though I smoked plenty, I ran up six flights of stairs. Lying in the dark land of the *cucarachas*, her Latin and Greek grammars flung into chaos, radio playing softly, my Sylvia waited, seething.

"I brought fried chicken, pickles, potato latkes, and mandel bread. Turn on the light. Sit up. My mother also knit a sweater for you." I always brought food back to MacDougal Street. Sylvia would eat.

Once, when I was at my parents' apartment, Sylvia phoned to say that she'd slit her wrists. She hadn't wanted me to go alone to visit my parents for a few hours, and she had refused to come with me.

I picked up the phone and said, "Hello, Sylvia?"

A tiny voice said, "I just slit my wrists."

I left my parents' apartment, but not before my mother had packed a bag with a dozen bagels, two jars of gefilte fish, and a salad she made of onions and radishes.

I didn't want to go rushing back to MacDougal Street, intimidated by Sylvia's threats of self-destruction or her announcement of the fait accompli. I didn't believe she had slit her wrists. But I couldn't be certain. (She had a small, fine, nearly imperceptible scar on one wrist, and claimed she'd once tried to kill herself.) In my frustration—refusing to be intimidated, yet feeling terrified—I became angry at my mother for detaining me as she packed food. She suspected things were bad on MacDougal Street, but if I left without the food she'd know they were very bad. I was ashamed and didn't want her to know how Sylvia and I lived, but I didn't want Sylvia to bleed to death. I waited for the food, then ran to the subway, then ran from the subway to MacDougal Street, through the crowds, up the six flights of stairs to our apartment, and I burst in hot and wild, the bag of food in my arms, shouting, "I don't give a damn if you slashed your neck."

She had sliced her wrists very superficially. Having done it before, she was good at it. There was almost no bleeding. There'd be no scars. She began picking at the food. She liked gefilte fish. It pleased me to see her eat. There was hope if Sylvia ate gefilte fish, homemade, delicious, nothing to fight about. She ate as if she were doing me a favor I didn't deserve.

Sylvia never read a newspaper. I told her what was happening. She didn't care one bit. I told her anyhow. She listened suspiciously, as if I had some dubious motive for obliging her to hear what I read in the newspaper. Mainly it was innocent chatter, but I admit I had a vague notion that mental health is more or less proportional to the attention you give to matters outside your head. It couldn't be bad for her to hear about politics, scientific developments, sports, art, fashion, crime, various disasters, etc. The worst news—if it's in a newspaper—probably didn't happen to you, and it offers a reassuringly normal connection to daily life. The world goes on. Earthquakes, fires, airplane crashes, murders—whatever else they may be—are news, part of the flow of days, weeks, eras.

I told Sylvia that Russian scientists said the core of the earth is pure iron, and the temperature, 1,800 miles down, is about 12,000 degrees centigrade, much hotter than had been supposed. I told her that Nina Simone is at the Village Gate, and Thelonius Monk is at the Jazz Gallery. I told her that an eighteen-year-old light heavyweight boxer, Cassius Clay, won a gold medal at the Rome Olympics; Rafer Johnson won the gold in the decathlon.

I read her the report about a New York magistrate, an early feminist, who ordered the names of two men put into the record in a vice case. He said, "You have the girls' names here. Put the men's names in, too." So the names Whitey Doe and Larry Doe were changed to Whitford May and L. Sleeper. Coincidentally, it was reported the same day that The International Society for the Welfare of Cripples changed its name to The International Society for the Rehabilitation of the Disabled.

I told Sylvia that Americans were dying in Vietnam. Every other week, in 1961, one of our military advisers was kidnapped, or an American contractor was shot. We were building airfields then and giving other forms of humanitarian aid to South Vietnam. Our efforts were impeded by the Viet Cong. Sylvia listened, and occasionally responded. I told her that a British physicist said Einstein's idea of matter as a form of energy, $E = MC^2$, was too simple. New atom-smashing technology had revealed that matter consisted of two major categories, leptons and baryons, which is to say light and heavy. Sylvia said, "He says Einstein is too simple?"

I told her that below the ice of Antarctica, huge trees had become coal, which meant the theory of continental drift was true; that Norell, an American designer, had introduced culottes—pants that looked like a skirt—for city street wear; and that American Orientalists had left for Egypt to save the temple of Ramses II from the waters of the Aswan High Dam, built by Russian engineers.

I wanted to see Marcel Marceau and his mime company at City Center, and *Krapp's Last Tape* at the Provincetown Playhouse, just down the street at 133 MacDougal. Sylvia enjoyed both performances. I had to make the suggestion, buy tickets, and, when it was time to leave for the theater, say, "Come on, come on, let's go. We'll be late."

She didn't like to commit herself, far in advance, to leaving the apartment at a particular moment. Who knows how you'll feel when the moment comes? Besides, it could be more pleasing to read reviews than actually go to a movie or a play.

I told Sylvia that Dr. Menges, professor of Central Asian languages at Columbia University, had been stopped by a gang of kids while taking his evening walk on Morningside Drive and knocked to the pavement with a heavy board. He rose, flailed at them with his cane. They ran away. He spoke to a reporter and was quoted at length. "I have traveled alone through the interior of the Caucasus . . . amid primitive tribes. I have gone among bandits. But in a so-called civilized city," he said, "near a large university, I am attacked by jungle beasts." It was clear he meant "Negroes." In the early sixties the word appeared with increasing frequency in the newspapers.

Awakened affectionately by Sylvia. She looked at my cigarettes beside the bed and said, "You shouldn't smoke so much. For my sake." I said, "I smoke because we fight." She began biting my arm. I yelled. She leaped out of bed and announced, "That's the beginning and the ending of a day." I lay there a long time. Finally, I dragged myself out of bed and turned on fire for coffee, got bread, honey, and an orange. Sylvia went back to bed and said, "You really take good care of yourself." I ate a slice of bread and put everything else back. Then I sat on the bed beside her. I was about to make amends. She sat up, slapped my face, and said, "Have a cigarette." Later, still in bed, me sitting beside her, Sylvia brought up the New Year's Eve party we'd gone to in the Brooklyn tenement. She said that when Willy Stark kissed her, she had turned her face at the last moment so that he kissed her on the cheek, not the lips. She said she should have necked with him so I could have seen it and had my evening ruined. I said, "I would have left and never seen you again." She said, "That's impossible. You love me. Besides, your mother would make you return to me."

(Journal, January 1961)

Almost all of our friends were Jewish, black, homosexual, more or less drug-addicted, very intelligent, very nervous, or a combination of two or three of these things. Willy Stark was from Mississippi, very black, very handsome. We met at the University of Michigan. When he moved to New York, we'd go out to jazz clubs and sit for hours, listening to the music, hardly talking. He never said very much. We heard Charlie Mingus at the Five Spot. Another time, we heard Miles Davis at Basin Street. It was a rainy night in the middle of the week, and there were few people in the audience. After one of Davis's solos, performed with his back to the audience, Willy whispered, "He's a poet." Though I couldn't say exactly what Willy had in mind, I was moved by his comment. The university hadn't made his feelings thin and literary. He'd been raised on a farm. He knew about guns, wild weather, snakes, jazz, and much else that was real. Compared to Willy, I considered myself effete. He hardly talked; I talked too much and too easily. He made me wonder if I'd believe the things I said, let alone think them in the first place, if I didn't get caught up in the momentum of talk. Sylvia never objected to me spending time with Willy. He was among the few exceptions to her rage.

Willy invited us to a New Year's Eve party in Brooklyn. At midnight, everyone kissing, Willy kissed Sylvia. Later, back on Mac-Dougal Street, as we fell asleep, Sylvia said he had wanted more than a kiss. "He said you wouldn't mind. He said you were hip."

She thought about Willy's kiss during the next few months, mentioning it several times, as if it had settled in her nervous system like a slow-growing virus. She also wanted more, at least in her fantasies, if not at the moment he kissed her. She said she'd turned her face away. That wasn't enough.

Willy worked as a counselor three days a week in a drug rehabilitation program for high school kids. On weekends, he sometimes made extra money by selling heroin, sharing the profits with a radical group in Ann Arbor. Willy had no politics, only tremendous anger. The radicals took to him. In his silence, they heard what they wanted to hear. They introduced Willy to a heroin source in Montreal, and gave him the money for his first buy. Heroin came by freighter from refineries in Bulgaria. Willy drove to Montreal, picked up the heroin, then drove back to New York.

He rented three or four apartments in Manhattan, and would arrange to meet his distributors in one of the apartments. He didn't tell them which apartment until the last minute. When they entered, the phone rang. It was Willy. He'd say they had ten minutes or so to get to another of his apartments. When they arrived there, the phone rang again, or else Willy was waiting with the heroin, a gun, and a bodyguard. If the distributors were two minutes late, Willy left. He believed that being punctual was crucial. He said, "If somebody's late, somebody's dead."

When he completed a sale, he flew to an island in the Caribbean, checked into a hotel, and stayed drunk until he stopped feeling frightened. A few times he rented a car and crashed into a tree or a wall. For some reason, it helped to free him of his fear. He told me all this after the kissing incident, as if to give me something personal and keep our friendship whole. He also offered me a chance to sell drugs. I was very touched, and actually thought about doing it. He said all I had to do was wear a suit and stand on a street corner with a briefcase. I said no. We didn't see each other again. Years later, I learned he had died of pancreatic cancer.

Through Willy, the healer-dealer, I had a sense of what it meant to be hip. He was my friend, but would have fucked Sylvia at the New Year's Eve party, if she'd let him, while I was in the next room. We sat together in jazz clubs for hours, saying almost nothing. I'd feel myself entering a trance of music, the meaning of this minute. How sad, or exciting, or weird it was to be alive in the sixties. I heard it in the jazz voices in the dark, smoky clubs. One night, at the bar in Birdland, with Willy beside me, we listened to Sarah Vaughan. She sang "Every little breeze seems to whisper Louise . . ." The wheeze in the rhyme of "breeze/Louise" vanished. She sang it out of existence, rendering only the exquisite mystery, such sweet and melancholy love as belonged to music in those days.

Because of our fights, Sylvia often didn't begin studying until after midnight. Sitting on the edge of the bed, remains of dinner all about, she held a grammar book in her lap and flipped pages, sometimes glaring at the words as if they were a distraction from her real concern—me. She said I was "doing this" to her, starting fights, trying to ruin her chances, make her fail. In fact I was proud of her, but it's true I was at least partly responsible for her suffering. I regretted having influenced her decision to study classics. She wasn't much interested in Latin and Greek, but she did the work because she feared academic disgrace, and, maybe, despite all the bad feeling, she wanted to please me. Night after night, she steeped herself in Homer and Virgil, a frenzy of mechanical performance that may have reminded her of her childhood schooling.

She'd been admitted to the Hunter elementary school for gifted children. Every morning, before leaving for school, she would go into the bathroom and vomit. Nobody at Hunter knew she lived in Queens, rather than Manhattan, where students were required to live, and she was constantly afraid that she would be discovered and publicly shamed. At the end of the day, she'd ride the subway back to Queens and sometimes fall asleep and miss her stop. She'd wake up, then catch a train going back. When she got home she'd find her mother flat on the floor, eyes shut, looking dead. It was a joke—she'd died waiting for Sylvia—but it frightened Sylvia.

I thought Sylvia went much too fast when she studied, flipping through pages she couldn't have absorbed, then tossing the book aside and picking up another. If there was tension between us—I'd made another hurtful remark, or I wanted to visit my parents, or I looked at a girl who passed us in the street—Sylvia would repeat to herself as she studied, "You're doing this to make me fail." Doing what? Sometimes, I knew what she had in mind; sometimes not. I never asked. She said, almost chanting, "You're doing this to make me fail," as the pages flipped by.

She'd say it again early in the morning as she flung out the door still wearing her clothes of the previous day, in which she'd slept, for maybe an hour, before leaving. Her long black hair bouncing and flying, blouse crumpled and half-buttoned, skirt twisted on her hips, she hustled through the Village streets to NYU, like a madwoman imitating a college student.

We were sitting on the bed after dinner. I was looking at a magazine. Sylvia was beginning to study. I commented on the beauty of one of the models in an advertisement. Sylvia glanced at the photo, then said, "Your ideal of beauty is blue, slanted eyes."

"So?"

Sylvia dropped backward on the bed, pulled the pillows against her ears, and began sobbing and thrashing. Then she stopped, sat up, and said, "I never went into detail about my sexual experiences."

I sat in silence and waited. She fell back again, made leering, hating faces, writhed like an epileptic, and then sat up and slapped my cheek and said, "I can't see why you don't adore me."

(*Journal, January 1961*)

In the throes of hysteria, her voice might suddenly become cool and elegant, and she'd make a witty remark, as if she were detached from herself and every quality of the moment was clear to her—the hatefulness of her display as well as my startled appreciation of her wit. I took this as a good sign, thinking it meant she wasn't really nuts. She felt the same way about it. "I know how I'm behaving," she'd say whenever I tried to talk to her about seeing a psychiatrist. She couldn't, then, see a psychiatrist. She knew herself; she couldn't talk about her excesses. Too shameful, too embarrassing.

Admiring the beauty of the model, an image in a magazine, meant I disliked Sylvia's looks and didn't love her. In casual chatter she heard inadvertent revelations of my true feelings. She was outraged. I loved the model. I'd said as much, damned myself.

Sylvia discovered an incapacitating, sentimental disease in me. Together, we nourished it. I wasn't a good enough person, I'd think, whereas she was a precious mechanism in which exceedingly fine springs and wheels had been brutally mangled by grief. Grief gave her access to the truth. If Sylvia said I was bad, she was right. I couldn't see why, but that's because I was bad. Blinded by badness.

She had to be right. I'd been living with her for months. I protected my investment, so to speak, by supposing that her hysteria and her accusations were not revolting and contemptible but a highly moral thing, like the paroxysm of an Old Testament prophet. They were fiery illuminations, moments of perverse grace. Not the manifestation of lunacy.

In a normal, defensive way, I'd also think nobody had ever talked to me as Sylvia did. That meant I wasn't bad, maybe. Nobody ever blamed me for having thoughts and feelings I didn't have. But even if I'd had bad thoughts and a generally nasty mental life, so what? Didn't I behave well? I was very affectionate, always touching. I came to believe the thoughts and feelings Sylvia hated in me were hers more than mine.

It would have been easy to leave Sylvia. Had it been difficult, I might have done it.

Repetition, according to religious thinkers, is seriousness. Working, eating, sleeping is repetition. The rising sun, phases of the moon, revolutions of planets and stars—everything in the universe repeats. Everything is ritual. To stop repeating is death—not the reverse. It was a fact of our daily life, as serious as our fights and compulsive sex, that we climbed six flights of stairs to and from the street. Our footsteps sounded in the resonant stairwell, day and night. To go to classes at NYU, Sylvia climbed twice, five times a week. I listened to her going. I heard her returning. To go to the grocery, movies, local bars, or the mailbox, we climbed six flights down, six flights up. To buy a pack of cigarettes required the same number of steps as when I went to visit my father in the hospital, in the intensive care unit, after his second heart attack. The doctors said my father also had prostate cancer, but they didn't want to operate in the summer.

"It's too hot." I told this to Sylvia. Instantly, she said, "In the winter it will be too cold." I was surprised by the pain her remark caused me. But of course she was right. I hadn't understood the doctors, or hadn't wanted to. They didn't think my father would survive an operation. There was no point in operating. He wouldn't live long enough to die of cancer. I had not understood.

The stairway was the spine of the building, the steps were vertebrae. I climbed through a body. It exuded odors and made noises. I smelled food cooking, incense burning, and the gases of hashish and roach poison. I heard radios and phonograph players, the old Italian lady who screamed "Bassano" every day, and the boy's footsteps running in the hall. Bassano never answered the old lady, presumably his grandmother, and I never once saw him. When I met her in the hallway or on the stairs, she always nodded and said, "Nice day," regardless of the weather.

At the landings, the hallway struck left and right toward the apartments. A light bulb burned at the landings where four toilets stood side by side, the doors shut. The toilets were closets about ten feet high, four feet wide, and six feet deep. Above the bowl was a water tank, it gurgled and clanked. When you finished, you pulled a chain. This wasn't the kind of toilet where people settled down with literature.

Because the street door didn't lock and anyone might enter the building, our toilet was sometimes used by strangers. Toilet doors locked from the inside with hook-and-eye latches. I once saw a ruby of brilliant blood gleaming on the toilet seat.

It had just been used by somebody to shoot up. Another time I opened the door on a boy and girl fucking. He sat on the bowl facing the door, his jeans and underwear around his ankles. She faced him, straddling his thighs, the divided flesh of her ass flaring. Her jeans and underwear lay in a pile. The boy stared over her left shoulder, his features squeezed by pleasure and strain. He stared directly at my eyes, oblivious to all but the feeling that beat in his cock. The girl was galloping hard. She didn't hear me open the door, didn't turn around, didn't lose the rhythm. I shut the door and hurried back to our apartment, told Sylvia. She said, "What if I need to use the toilet? I don't want to find people in there." She ordered me to tell them to get out or we'd call the police. I didn't want to. She didn't really want to either, but she'd taken a proprietary stand, her bourgeois dignity—of which she had none—was at stake. "If you don't go tell them," she said, "I will."

We went together.

I opened the door. The couple was gone.

Mother phoned just to talk, got Sylvia. Sylvia said she'd cut her hair badly, was too upset to talk, gave the phone to me.

Mother said, "How is Sylvia's finger?"

I said, "Nothing is wrong with her finger."

"No? She told me she cut her finger."

"No. It's her hair," I said. "She cut her hair badly. She doesn't like the way it looks."

"Oh, I thought she cut her finger. I was worried. Daddy heard and he was also aggravated."

He must have heard through mental telepathy. My mother sounded confused, intimidated by Sylvia.

Hurt, insulted, confused, my mother doesn't understand why Sylvia dislikes her. She is helpless to do anything about it. Her greatest worry was that I might marry a *shikse*. Nothing to worry about.

(Journal, January 1961)

A main cause of our fights was my desire to get off the bed after dinner and go into the tiny room adjoining the living room. It contained a cot, a kitchen chair, and a shaky wooden table where I set my typewriter. The table was shoved against the tall window, leaving only inches between the back of my chair and the cot. I sat at the table, looking out over the rooftops, with their chimneys, clotheslines, water tanks, and pigeon coops, toward the Hudson River and the Upper West Side. If I looked down, I looked into the bedroom windows of a tenement about fifty feet away. Winds from the west rattled the window glass, penetrating old loose putty, carrying icy air from the Hudson River to my fingers. They stiffened as I typed. My chin and the tip of my nose became numb. I'd hear Sylvia sigh and flip the pages of her books. I could hear the sound of her pencil when she made notes. I was four steps away. Nevertheless, she'd feel abandoned, excluded, lonely, angry, and God knows what else. Only four steps away, but I was out of sight and not seeing her. She may have felt herself ceasing to exist. She didn't want me to go into the cold room.

After dinner I lingered with her on the bed, reading a magazine as she collected notebooks, preparing to study. When she began to study, I'd begin to leave the bed. I never just left in a simple, natural way, but always with vague gradualness, letting Sylvia get used to the idea. I'd stir, lay aside the magazine, lean toward the cold room.

"Going to your hole?"

Sometimes I'd settle back onto the bed, thinking, "I'll write tomorrow when she's at school. Maybe she'll go to sleep in a few hours. I'll write then. A small sacrifice. Better than a fight." That in itself—my desire not to fight—could be an incitement. "Why don't we discuss this for a minute . . ." To sound rational, when she was wrought up, wrought her up further, like a smack in the face. She once threw the typewriter she'd given me—"To help you write"—at my head. An Olivetti portable, Lettera 22. It struck a wall, then the floor, but was undamaged. I still use it. She also failed to destroy the telephone, though she often tried, knocking it off the shelf, or flinging it against the brick wall.

I wrote and I wrote, and I tore up everything, and I wrote some more. After a while I didn't know why I was writing. My original desire, complicated enough, became a grueling compulsion, partly in spite of Sylvia. I was doing hard work in the cold room, much harder than necessary, in the hope that it would justify itself.

Writing a story wasn't as easy as writing a letter, or telling a story to a friend. It should be, I believed. Chekhov said it was easy. But I could hardly finish a page in a day. I'd find myself getting too involved in the words, the strange relations of their sounds, as if there were a music below the words, like the weird singing of a demiurge out of which came images, virtual things, streets and trees and people. It would become louder and louder, as if the music were the story. I had to get myself out of the way, let it happen, but I couldn't. I was a bad dancer, hearing the music, dancing the steps, unable to let the music dance me.

Writing in the cold room, I'd sometimes become exhilarated, as if I'd transcended all difficulties, done something good. The story had written itself. It bore no residual trace of me. It was clean. A day later, rereading with a more critical eye, I sank into the blackest notions of my fate. I'd wanted so little, just a story that wouldn't make me feel ashamed of myself next week, or five years from now. It was too much to want. The story I'd written was no good. It broke my heart. I was no good.

"Going to your hole?"

I felt I was digging it.

Sylvia had a pain in her shoulder. She lay in bed and asked me to rub it, but when I touched her she squirmed spasmodically and pushed my hand away. I kept trying do it right, but she wouldn't stop squirming and wouldn't tell me just where to rub. Then she lunged out of bed and paced the room, rubbing her shoulder herself.

"I have a sore spot. A stranger could rub it better than you."

(Journal, January 1961)

Sylvia was often in pain or a nervous, defeated condition, especially when she got her period. She'd lie on the couch, our bed, groaning, whimpering, begging me to go buy her Tampax. I didn't see how it could ease her pain, but she was insistent, whining and writhing. She needed Tampax. This invariably happened very late, long after midnight, when I was thinking about going to sleep. Instead of sleeping, I'd be out in the streets looking for an open drugstore. I dreaded the man at the counter, who would think I was an exceptionally bizarre Village transvestite. I asked for Tampax in a hoodlumish voice, as if it were manufactured for brutal males. One night, when I returned to the apartment with the box of Tampax, I detected the faintest smile on Sylvia's lips. Having me buy her Tampax turned her on. I decided never to do it again. As if she'd read my mind, she stopped asking.

How much else was theater? Sylvia knew how she was behaving. She didn't want to discuss it with a psychiatrist. Too embarrassing and there was no point. Maybe everything was theater. The difference between one person and another lay in what they knew about their private theaters. Willy Stark had some idea like that: everything is theater; nothing is real. Everybody had a role to play; or, everybody, like it or not, had to play a role. You played in your theater, or in somebody else's, depending on your willpower and imagination. Around then, in Jerusalem, Adolf Eichmann was telling the world that he'd never killed a Jew or a non-Jew. Killing wasn't in his nature. But, he said, if he'd been ordered from high up in the SS to kill his father, he'd have done it.

Sylvia looks in the mirror and dreams about lovers as she cuts her hair. She worries about pimples, pains, and pregnancy, and she worries about what everyone thinks of her, and she spends a lot of time sleeping, or lying about eating candy and frosted rolls, complaining of pains. Occasionally, she will show me affection. She went on today about her periods, how much of her life has bled away.

(Journal, January 1961)

I recorded our fights in a secret journal because I was less and less able to remember how they started. There would be an inadvertent insult, then disproportionate anger. I would feel I didn't know why this was happening. I was the object of terrific fury, but what had I done? What had I said? Sometimes I would have the impression that the anger wasn't actually directed at me. I'd merely stepped into the line of fire, the real target being long dead. I wasn't him. He wasn't me. I'd somehow become Sylvia's hallucination. Perhaps I didn't really exist, at least not the way a table, a hat, or a person exists. Once, when I thought a bad scene was over, I lay down and threw my arm over my eyes. It was after 3 a.m., but Sylvia refused to turn off the light. She sat in a chair, six feet from the bed, and watched me. Then I heard her say, "I don't know how you find the courage to go to sleep." She might stick a knife in my heart, I supposed. But she couldn't afford to kill me. She'd be alone. Sleep took no courage.

Another time she pulled all my shirts out of the dresser and threw them on the floor and jumped up and down on them and spit on them. I seized her wrists and pressed her down on the bed while I shouted into her face that I loved her. By tiny degrees, she seemed to relax, to relent. I urged her along, more observer than committed fighter, and I sensed the changes she passed through, each degree of feeling.

After a fight, unless there was sex, Sylvia usually collapsed into sleep. Ringing with anguish, exceedingly awake, I forced myself to rethink the fight, moment by moment, writing it all down in the cold room as Sylvia slept. It was my way of knowing, if nothing else, that this was really happening. It was also a way of talking about it, though only to myself. I hid the journal in a space just below the surface of the table where I wrote stories. None of the stories were about life on MacDougal Street. My life wasn't subject matter. It wasn't to be exploited for the purpose of fiction. I'd never even talked about it to anyone, and I imagined that nobody knew how bad things were. As a matter of high principle and shame, I kept everything that happened on MacDougal Street to myself. By sneaking the events into my journal, when Sylvia collapsed, I made them seem even more secret. Then, one afternoon, Malcolm Raphael, another old friend from the University of Michigan, visited. We were alone in the apartment. He said he'd just come from Majorca, where he'd overheard some Americans, lying near him on the beach, talking about me and Sylvia. One of them lived in our building. He described our fights to the others.

I felt myself going blind and deaf, repudiating the news, denying it in my physiology. It was like fainting. Malcolm saw my reaction, laughed, and told me about fights he'd had with his wife. It was an extraordinary moment. Men never talked to each other this way. His fights were as bad as mine, but he made them seem funny. He was unashamed.

I was grateful to him, relieved, giddy with pleasure. So others lived this way, too, even a charming, sophisticated guy like Malcolm. We laughed together. I felt happily irresponsible. Countless men and women, I supposed, all over America, were tearing each other to pieces. How great. I was normal. It was a delightful feeling, but to think this way also gave me the creeps. I was reminded of some former acquaintances, flamboyant gay kids I'd met years ago, while learning how to skate at Iceland, the rink next to Madison Square Garden. I'd find them speeding about, slashing ice, or gathered at the edge of the rink watching the skaters and gossiping. They referred to everyone as a "faggot." The cop we passed in the street was a "cop-faggot." The mayor of New York was a "mayor-faggot." A famous football player was a "football-faggot." Every "he" was a "she." The more manly, strict, correct, official, moral, authoritative, the more faggot she.

Now, after listening to Malcolm, I felt like the gay kids—shame notwithstanding—on stage, my secret life subject to the voracious curiosity of everybody, and in their gayish manner, I let myself think every man and woman who lived together were like Sylvia and me. Every couple, every marriage, was sick. Such thinking, like bloodletting, purged me. I was miserably normal; I was normally miserable. Whatever people thought of me, I could think it first of them. I could flaunt my shame as a form of contempt for others. No better disguise for shame than contempt, and nothing is easier to do than to sneer and denigrate. Nothing is more pleasing to the vanity of others. Any two people chatting are making invidious remarks about a third. It is a perverse form of generosity, and self-adoration.

Sylvia knew nothing about the gossip. Since she lived in constant fear of humiliation, I didn't tell her. The fact that our cover was blown strengthened my commitment to her. She'd really been hurt, virtually killed, even if she didn't know it. We weren't yet married, but Sylvia wanted to do it soon, and the simple idea that it would be unwise for us to marry did not occur to me. If I did not want to marry Sylvia, I couldn't think I didn't, couldn't let myself know it. I had no thoughts or feelings that weren't moral. When I added two and two, a certain moral sensation arrived with the number four.

Sylvia complained again of a swollen spot on the back of her neck. I rubbed the area for a little while. I felt nothing swollen. Anyhow, the complaining stopped. I then said I wanted to go do some work. She said she had a stomachache. I didn't believe her, and I despised myself for not believing her. She needed comfort. Whether or not she had real pain was irrelevant. She lay on her stomach and moaned in different ways, emitted small shrieks. I asked her to stop, turned her over. She moaned through bared teeth, her eyes wide and fixed on mine. I cupped her mouth. She bit my hand, then sobbed and said I could go. She wanted me to go. I could continue living with her if I liked, but I was also free to go. She let me hold her. I cried a little, kissing her, holding her. I showed love, but it felt like a self-accusation, or an apology. That was my apology—very sincere—but it was for nothing specific. Like a religious convulsion. You apologize for being alive, for not being sick, for not being physically deformed, for not being as bad off as other people. I don't know what I apologized for. Maybe for the love I desecrated by not believing in Sylvia's pain. I felt utterly sincere, apologizing, kissing her. It was too delicious, I think.

(Journal, March 1961)

I was affected by cultural radiations from newspapers, radio, movies, television, but my life was MacDougal Street, voices through the walls, traffic noises through the windows, odors floating up the stairwell, and always Sylvia. A visit to my parents lasted only a few hours. There was no place to go where I might forget MacDougal Street and Sylvia for a little while.

With few exceptions, Sylvia imagined my friends were her enemies. Once, hurrying back to the apartment from a twenty-minute meeting with a friend in the San Remo bar, a hundred feet from the entrance to our building, I opened the apartment door on madness. Sylvia, at the stove, five feet away, turned toward me holding a plate of spaghetti in her hand—already startling, since she never cooked—and the plate came sailing toward my face, strands of spaghetti untangling like a ball of snakes. "Dinner," she said. I caught it against my forearm.

She'd been enraged by my meeting downstairs, so she cooked spaghetti. Why? She saw herself standing at the stove and cooking spaghetti like a woman who does such things for a man. The man, however, being viciously ungrateful, abandoned her. While Sylvia slaved over a boiling pot of spaghetti, I regaled myself with conversation and a glass of beer. In a bitterly hideous way, it struck me as funny, but I wasn't laughing.

The telephone, if it rang for me, was also her enemy. She'd say, "His master's voice," and hand me the phone. After I put it down, she'd jeer, "You love Bernie, don't you?" He was a witty guy. I'd laughed too hard at his remarks during the phone call, and Sylvia resented all that flow of feeling in his direction. Eventually, when answering the phone, if Sylvia was in the room, I kept my voice even and dull, or edged with annoyance, as if the call were tedious. I learned to talk in two voices, one for the caller, the other for Sylvia, who listened nearby in the tiny apartment, storing up acid criticisms.

I liked Sylvia's friends, and I was glad when they phoned or visited. They proved Sylvia was lovable, and they let me believe that we were good company. I wanted Sylvia to have lots of friends, but she was carefully selective and soon got rid of her prettiest girlfriends, keeping only those who didn't remind her of her physical imperfections. In a department store, if a saleslady merely told Sylvia that a dress was too long for her, she took it as a comment on her repulsive shortness. If a saleslady said bright yellow was wrong for Sylvia, it was a judgment on her repulsive complexion. She would quickly drag me out into the street, telling me that I thought the same as the saleslady.

"Why don't you admit it?" she said.

If the saleslady was affectionate and sincerely attentive, Sylvia would buy anything from her. For every hundred dollars she spent on clothes, she got about fifty cents in value, and would have done better, at much less cost, in a Salvation Army thrift shop, blindfolded. When she liked some piece of clothing and felt good wearing it—a certain cashmere sweater, a cotton blouse, or her tweed coat with the torn sleeve—she'd wear it for days. She'd sleep in it.

Saturday was spent making up for Friday. We slept, made love, ate. I didn't write, she didn't study. We tried to sleep again, couldn't sleep. Made love. Not well, but exhaustingly. She said, "You're not natural." We slept.

(Journal, March 1961)

My mother's way of trying to help was to send food. I carried large grocery bags of bagels, fried chicken, potato latkes, cakes, and cookies to MacDougal Street. My father's way was silence and looks of sad philosophical concern, which was no help, but he also gave me money. Our expenses were low, forty dollars a month for rent, maybe a little more for the food we kept in the refrigerator where it would be safe from roaches—spaghetti, oranges, eggs, coffee, milk, bread, and the pastries Sylvia loved. Gas and electric cost us about ten or eleven dollars a month.

The one time I tried to tell my father about my life with Sylvia, I became incoherent and suffered visibly. As in a dream,

I couldn't seem to say what I intended. My mouth felt weak and too big, my words sloppy. But he understood. Even before I did, he understood I was asking for his permission to do something terrible. He cut me off, saying, "She's an orphan. You cannot abandon her." A plain moral law. He couldn't bear listening to me, seeing my torment. So he didn't allow discussion, didn't let me speak evil. Then he told about the wretchedness of husbands. He knew a man, seventy-seven years old, an immigrant Jew from Poland with a butcher shop on Hester Street, whose wife told the FBI he was a communist. They investigated him, and he spent nine days in jail. Fortunately, his name was good in the neighborhood. He wasn't a communist. I got the point. Wives might do bad things to their husbands, but nothing could or should be done to end the miseries of the couple. The couple is absolute, immutable as the sea and the shore. With his little story, my father condemned me to marriage.

I'd wanted him to say something, but not that. I went away lonely and wretched. More than ever, I had to talk to somebody and I wondered about seeing a psychiatrist. In graduate school, I had read an essay on Jonathan Swift by the psychoanalyst Phyllis Greenacre. It was well written and, unlike much psychoanalytic writing, seemed conscious of literary values. Maybe I could talk to her. I thought about what I could say or dare not say. Finally, I dialed her number. She gave me an appointment.

Her living room was her office. A big room, with chairs and couches covered by lovely fabrics. The atmosphere was entirely domestic and pleasant, not the least medical. Had people come here to rave about their miserable lives? There were literary magazines, like the *Hudson Review,* on a coffee table. I felt out of place, not so much that I'd brought misery to this lovely room, but that I lacked the cultivation necessary to discuss my ugly case. Again I was having trouble talking. How could I say what brought me here? Where would I find the words? Where would I begin? Then I noticed Greenacre was suffering from an attack of hay fever, and it became hard to think about anything else. She was on the verge of sneezing, sniffling constantly, pressing tissues to her nose, trying to look at me through teary eyes. Her head was full of turbulent waters. It was discouraging.

I began by apologizing for not being able to talk objectively about my problems. I said I wasn't sure I could get things right, or even review the events of my story correctly—what came first, what next. It was important, I said, no matter what I might say, not to misjudge Sylvia. I didn't want to make her sound like something she wasn't. Greenacre should be suspicious of every word I uttered. It was probably all lies. I'd try to tell the truth, but it was probably going to be a lie. My life, after all, wasn't a story. It was just moments, what happens from day to day, and it didn't mean anything, and there was no moral. I was unhappy, but that was beside the point, not that there was a point. I couldn't be objective. I couldn't be correct. I'd be entertaining, maybe, because that's how I was. A fool. Greenacre interrupted:

"Just talk. Don't worry about being objective."

Her remark was very brutal, I thought; also embarrassing. She seemed not to appreciate how I'd been struggling to make clear the difficulty, for me, in saying anything, and therefore how amazing it was that I'd come this far, sitting here with a doctor, trying desperately to make it understood that I could never make anything clear, and the entire enterprise was worthless. Suddenly—jolted by her brutal interruption—I heard myself. I'd merely bumbled for five minutes. I'd been boring. I'd frustrated the doctor. If I had only this incoherent stuff to offer, she couldn't do her job. I was virtually demented.

She waited, also struggling, if not against boredom then against hay fever for composure and concentration.

I then plunged ahead; talked for fifty minutes, withholding a little, but without being incoherent. She sniffled and responded to nothing, just took it all in. At the end, she said Sylvia and I both needed psychoanalysis. She would recommend someone, if I liked. She was no longer practicing, only acting as a consultant.

I asked if she had any idea about Sylvia and me, any impression she might be able to give me. She seemed reluctant to say another word. But I'd come across, told her so much. I was going to pay for the hour. With a shrug and a dismissive tone, she said, "You're feeding on each other."

Toward the end of our time on MacDougal Street, I convinced Sylvia to visit a psychiatrist at Columbia Neuropsychiatric. A friend of Sylvia's had been seeing him, and he said the doctor knew his business and was a decent guy. Sylvia let me make an appointment for her. The day of the appointment, Sylvia refused to get out of bed. I begged her. I argued and cajoled and yelled. Finally, I ran out the door, down the stairs, and hailed a taxi. I went to the appointment. It was extremely embarrassing. I explained as best I could. The doctor let me talk, listened to me for about an hour and a half. For the first time, I had no trouble talking. The bad scene with Sylvia before leaving the apartment, and the wild rush uptown, had thrust me into the middle of our saga. I talked about what happened minutes ago and what was happening day after day. I talked rapidly and lucidly, and I produced a voluminously detailed picture. At last, as if he'd heard something crucial, he said, "Has she started calling you a homosexual?" I told him about the Tampax. He said this is very serious. Sylvia ought to be committed. If I'd sign papers, he'd do the rest. He followed me to the head of the stairs, calling after me, "This is very serious."

Maybe I'd wanted to hear him say something like that. Whether or not we were "feeding on each other" was less important than the fact that Sylvia was certifiably, technically nuts. This knowledge was horribly exciting. It made me very high. I ran to the subway, sobbing a little, running back to my madwoman. I'd been strengthened by new, positive knowledge, and a sense of connection to the wisdom of our healing institutions. As a result, nothing changed.

Awakened by a phone call. Sylvia, in a hurry to go to school, asks for the mailbox key on her way out the door. I say, "Will you let me know if I got any mail?" She says, "No. I need something to read during class." She leaves. I hang up the phone. She comes back carrying a letter from my brother. She says, "Can I read it?" I say, "No." She says, "Why not?" I say, "He might have intended it for me." She shouts, stomps the floor, pulls the door shut with a great bang, runs down the stairs. I make coffee and gobble up half a loaf of bread without slicing it, tearing off wads, smearing the wads with butter, jamming them into my mouth.

(Journal, March 1961)

One evening, after another long fight, Sylvia went raging out of the apartment to take an exam in Greek, saying she would fail, she had no hope of passing, she would fail disgracefully, it was my fault, and "I will get you for this." The door slammed. I sat on the bed listening to her footsteps hurry down the hall, then down the stairs. I was immobilized by self-pity, and, as usual, unable to remember how the fight had started, or even what it was about except that Sylvia was going to tell my parents about me, and report me to the police, and she would do something personally, too. In a spasm of strange determination, I got up, went out the door, and followed her through the streets to NYU. I was stunned and blank, but moving, crossing streets, walking through the park, then joining a crowd of students and entering the main building of NYU, following Sylvia down a hallway, up a flight of stairs, and down another hallway to her exam room. I stood outside the room and looked in. She sat in the last row and hadn't removed her thin, brown leather wraparound winter coat, its tall collar standing higher than her ears. The coat was nothing against a New York winter, but Sylvia thought she looked great in it and wore it constantly, even on the coldest days. She was bent, huddled over the questions printed on her exam paper, as if the exam itself delivered heavy blows to her shoulders and the top of her head. Her ballpoint pen, clutched in a bloodless fist, moved very quickly, her face close to the page, breathing on the words she wrote. Five minutes after the hour, she surrendered the paper to her professor and came out of the room with a yellowish face, looking killed. When she saw me, she came to me without seeming in the least surprised, and whispered that she had been humiliated, had failed, it was my fault. But her tone was not reproachful. She leaned against me a little as we started away from the room. I could feel how glad she was to find me waiting for her. I put my arm around her. She let me kiss her. We walked home together, my arm around her, keeping her warm.

Her exam was the best in the class, and the professor urged her to persist in classical studies. She was pleased, more or less, but whatever she felt lacked the depth and intensity of her feelings before the exam. Her pleasure in being praised had no comparable importance, no comparable meaning. The success wasn't herself. It had no necessity, like the shape of her hands or knees. It didn't matter to her.

She didn't always do that well; but considering how we lived, it was a miracle she passed any course. She took no pride in her success and never exhibited her learning in conversation, never referred to it. She was basically uninterested; only performing. Academic achievements, to her, were an embarrassment.

"I'd give thirty points off my IQ for a shorter nose."

"Nothing is wrong with your nose."

"It's too long, a millimeter too long."

Agatha Seaman, who lived in Yonkers and visited Sylvia regularly, told her about a doctor in Switzerland who could reshape her nose without surgery, molding it by hand over a period of weeks at his clinic in the Alps, where you could also ski and the meals were marvelous. "Everybody goes there." Sylvia cared less about the shape of her nose than its length, but she yearned for the mythical doctor. He'd been mentioned in a fashion magazine and described as the darling of European society. Sylvia was resentful of Agatha, because she could easily afford to spend weeks at the alpine clinic. Not that Sylvia would go if she could afford it. Still, she wanted to believe there was such a doctor, and hope existed for her nose, and it was available to her, not just Agatha.

I liked Sylvia's nose, but I said nothing, certainly nothing about the fantasy doctor. I might easily say the wrong thing. My idea was that Sylvia wanted someone to do to her nose what she did to her dresses, which was to change them. She changed their length or width, or removed a collar or added a collar or tightened the shoulders. She always ruined her dresses, or else she decided, after much cutting and sewing, that the changes didn't work for her. There were dozens of beautiful dresses and skirts, purchased with inheritance money soon after her mother's death. None of them fit like another. They were stuffed into boxes and suitcases that were jammed under the couch and in the back of the closet and almost never opened. She wore only a few things and she had no memory of the extent of her wardrobe, no idea of how many thousands of dollars she had spent on clothes. Since she often fell asleep in her clothes—too depressed or too lazy to undress, or because she felt good in what she was wearing—she wore the same thing for days while hundreds of pieces of clothing, altered and realtered, were simply forgotten and never worn.

I hoped that she'd leave her nose alone. As for Agatha's doctor, he was like everything else in her life, an extravagant fantasy somehow related to boys. Agatha was subject to passionate fixations on boys, always younger than she, and always poor, ignorant, dark—Arab, Turk, Italian, Puerto Rican—sublimely handsome, and invariably vicious. If they weren't vicious when they met Agatha, she helped them discover it in themselves. Then she told Sylvia about it. Sylvia told me. Month after month, I heard about the boys.

Sprawling for hours on our couch, Agatha would tell Sylvia exceedingly detailed stories about the boys—how last night she waited in an alley behind the hotel where Abdul or Francisco or Julio worked as a bellhop or a busboy, and when he appeared after work, she surprised him. The boys were outraged by these surprises, but Agatha always brought gifts—jewelry, leather jackets, luscious silk shirts—tickets of admission to their lives. Trembling with humility and fear, she held the gift toward the boy. Unable to reject it, he relented, and she'd follow him down the street as he fondled the gift, maybe tried it on. Sylvia imitated Agatha imitating herself, whimpering about how gorgeous he looked, how she'd been absolutely right, "Magenta was Abdul's color" or "Francisco looked divine in black silk."

Gradually, the boy's anger gave way to a different, yet related feeling. The boy would lead Agatha into a doorway or a phone booth where he might allow her to blow him. Sometimes he'd turn her around and abuse her from behind, then leave her burning and bleeding and go to meet his real date. Agatha referred to the boy's date as "a mean selfish bitch." With monotonic matter-of-factness, she told Sylvia exactly what the boys did to her. She never seemed to notice that her stories always followed the same pattern—passionate fixation, gifts, debasement, abandonment. Her stories were true, I think, but so much the same it began to seem Agatha was enslaved by the pattern, living to do it again and again and to tell Sylvia that it had happened again. Telling about it was masturbatory, but just as important as the real experience; maybe more important, or maybe there was no difference any longer for Agatha. She and Sylvia would lie about for hours, sometimes drawing portraits of each other as they drank tea and Agatha told her story. They looked beautifully civilized in their intimacy.

Agatha, always giving the boys gifts, might have been a gift sufficient in herself—a slender blonde about the same size and shape as Sylvia—but she indulged an enervated, unattractive manner. Her voice, kept low and dull to suggest feminine reserve, suggested instead a low-voltage brain and morbidity. Her complexion, embalmed for years in cosmetic chemicals, had the texture of tofu.

Contempt, pity, prurient fascination, and affection bound Sylvia to Agatha. I liked her, too, and also felt the other things. She had a sickly, languid manner, making her seem physically weak, and an air of fear and injury, which gave her the appeal of a doomed kitten. A small face with light blue staring eyes; a small mouth with lips that hardly moved when she talked.

Nobody was more harmless or perversely exciting. The boys sometimes beat up Agatha, but she never seemed to bruise or scar, at least not visibly. There was no tension in her. Nothing resisted; nothing broke.

Despite righteous anger at the terrible boys, and sympathy for Agatha, it was impossible not to taste their nasty gratification. Her very harmlessness invoked torturers. Being rich and pampered was already potentially offensive. The expensive gifts, which the boys were unable to reject, pleased them and compromised them at once. In some strange way, the gifts seemed to beg for a return in affectionate cruelty. The boys did what she wanted them to do. They served her need to grovel, to feel pain, to collect experience for her stories. Otherwise, nothing happened to Agatha. She spent hours and hours shopping, but, aside from the time she spent with boys, she didn't seem to live. She never had a conversation with anyone that she thought was worth repeating. She was never impressed by anything in Paris or Rome or wherever she vacationed; at least she never said what she'd seen or done in Europe unless it had to do with boys. She never mentioned a book. She did nothing athletic aside from the few sexual contortions in which she accommodated boys. She did go to movies, but she was never able to remember what the movies had been about, only what the actors looked like and maybe what they wore.

Nevertheless, she always had something to talk about. Lying on the couch in our small, roach-infested apartment, wearing the smartest frock from the smartest shop, Agatha produced her tales of abomination. It was her life. She was interested in almost nothing. She had everything she wanted. Every pleasure, every pain. From smart shop to sleazy joint, the limp, colorless bit of girl burned along the extremest cutting edge of the sixties until her mother had her committed to a Manhattan madhouse. When Sylvia heard it cost several hundred dollars a day, she was outraged. She didn't want to visit Agatha, but finally the old feelings returned.

Agatha received us in a clean gray room—empty except for a bed, a table with a flower vase, and a chair—with barred windows, high above the city. She looked even softer and more languid. She looked chastened into quiet, spiritual composure. It was indeed a look. Plain and pure and holy. It was also sexy. The look was Agatha's, not a designer's. Basic Agatha, the look of her soul, her true, plain being. All connection with her former self, and the material world of glamour and depravity, had been severed. She looked good, and also like a good person.

We asked how she felt living in the hospital, incarcerated, under constant scrutiny. She answered by naming celebrities who had stayed in this hospital, and then she talked about several young people, presently among the inmates, who were marvelously interesting. She'd fallen among sensitive kids like herself. Artists, really, not lunatics. She had many new friends.

We'd gone to the hospital feeling pity for her. It was a cold dark day, and we'd had to walk against the wind for blocks and blocks, but it seemed necessary and decent to be doing this for Agatha. We felt good about ourselves. When we left the hospital the wind instantly reminded us of the painful streets, and we didn't feel good anymore; we laughed at ourselves and hurried home feeling annoyed and foolish, like poor ignorant folks who'd had no idea that a hospital, even with bars on the windows, might be chic and fascinating. Agatha loved the place, was in no hurry to leave. She stayed about five weeks and came out a lesbian, having met and fallen in love with a wonderful crazy girl who treated her badly.

Only about twenty days before the wedding and we had a fight. Not worse than other fights but, the wedding so close, it felt more bitter, more wrong. I tried to get Sylvia out of bed at 8 a.m., when the alarm went off. She shrieked, slapped the blanket, demanded to be let alone. I cuddled and rocked her, trying very gently to get her out of bed. It was important to me—since we are getting married—that we begin trying to live in a normal, regular way. She knew what I thought, took it as a criticism. Refused to get up. Around noon she got up and said she wanted to buy some bras and a wedding dress. She wanted me to go with her. She insisted I go with her. I said I needed a shave; didn't want to walk into a women's clothing store looking the way I did. The truth is I didn't want to go. She said it didn't matter how I looked. I shaved. We went. It was very windy and burning cold. She said that if she'd known how cold it was, she wouldn't have insisted that I go with her. In a store on Eighth Street, she tried on two dresses. The first was red with a flat neck. It set off her complexion, eyes, and hair. She looked nice, but a red dress didn't look right for a wedding. I don't know why she bothered putting it on. Maybe she thought this dress would be an exception, as if there were a kind of red that a bride might wear. She did look good in it. The second dress was yellow and had a flared skirt. It made her look rather wide, and it brought out yellowish tones in her skin. Later, she said that my face had been ugly with disapproval in the clothing store. "You know I'm a pig, and I know I'm a pig," she said. In the apartment again, she sat on the bed in her coat. Nothing had been accomplished. She hadn't bought bras or a wedding dress. I said, "Let's clean up this place." She said, "Yes." Her answer raised my spirits and I began to move about, picking things up. She noticed my show of energy, my optimism. She collapsed onto the bed, still in her coat, and she closed her eyes and started to go to sleep. I think I knew, before she collapsed, that I'd made a big mistake. My bustling about wouldn't inspire Sylvia to do the same. But I couldn't stop myself. It was my way of being insensitive, pretending not really to know her feelings, my way of not loving her. Seeing her lie there, in her coat, I quit trying to clean up. It was all very depressing, my stupid bustling and her collapse. I was more conscious than ever before of the havoc in our apartment, and in my heart. She keeps telling me that I think she is a pig. She doesn't like her face, doesn't like her body. I don't want to love her anymore. Too hard. I'm not good enough.

(Journal, March 1961)

We went to the Village Vanguard, about five or six blocks from MacDougal Street, to see Lenny Bruce. The room was jammed and very dark. You couldn't make out the ceiling, or the faces of people who stood along the bar. Hardly enough light for the waiters to pass between the tables. Light seemed concentrated in the spotlight on Lenny Bruce.

He wore a black leather jacket and had a hunched, scrawny, unwholesome, ratlike ferocity. His face, flattened and drained by the spotlight, looked hard, a poolroom face, not an entertainer. He began by reading a letter from a priest. It said Lenny Bruce is a moral genius, a great satirist. After reading the letter, Bruce began a routine made up mainly of shock words. He said, "nigger," "kike," "spic," while pointing to people in the audience. The audience tittered, laughed, then laughed more—and then—laughed as if we'd all gone over the edge, crazed by the annihilation of proprieties, or whatever had kept us from this until now. But Sylvia wasn't laughing. She smiled tentatively, as if more frightened than amused.

Bruce said a word like "nigger" had power because it was suppressed. He spoke quickly. Nothing must be suppressed? We musn't keep ourselves from knowing how depraved we are. At once scary and hilarious, he seemed to make sense. Who could resist him? A hysterically funny dead-white rat-face attacked political hypocrisies and puritanical attitudes toward sex. He did a long routine on the word "snot." The word became the thing. He said imagine it on the sleeve of his suede jacket, shining, stiff, impossible to remove. He rushed toward the audience with the medal of snot on his sleeve. People shrieked with pleasure. Another routine was about a lady selling cosmetics, the Avon Lady, who came to Bruce's house. She wanted to speak to his wife, who was in the bedroom, lying naked and unconscious in bed, sleeping off some drug. Bruce described himself dashing into the bedroom to make his wife presentable. He hung galoshes on her feet. Then he led the Avon Lady into the room. The audience laughed and screamed. In another routine, about an auto accident, Bruce made a picture of a man being lifted from a mangled car, half dead, bleeding heavily, in terrible pain. As he is carried to an ambulance, this man cannot help studying the beautiful ass of a nurse. The audience laughed and screamed. I laughed as much as anyone and felt a pleasing terror, like leaping from a high place. Now Sylvia was in tears, like a child, helpless with amazement, laughing. Our waiter stood beside our table, doubled over as if broken, clutching himself about the middle, paralyzed. Another waiter appeared and said, "Every fucking night this happens to you," and put his arm around him and led him away, still doubled over, broken by laughter.

Sylvia said she didn't do well on the Greek test. She was wildly remorseful. Wouldn't have sex. Got out of bed to brush her teeth, then had a small crying fit at the kitchen sink, and said, "I don't want to get married."

I lay there thinking that it will make my parents miserable if I call off the wedding. I will have disappointed them again. I will fail in everything and Sylvia will go completely nuts. Then I thought we will get married, and I will bring our child with me when I visit Sylvia in the nuthouse.

I won't go mad. Not me. Mindless sanity sustains me. I am an ordinary person. I don't know Latin or Greek. All I know is how to work. I went to my room and sat at the typewriter. My feet began to freeze, my knees felt numb. There was a steady crash of wind and rain against the window. Sylvia went back to bed. She might sleep until morning, I thought.

(Journal, March 1961)

In those days R. D. Laing and others sang praises to the condition of being nuts, and French intellectuals argued for allegiance to Stalin and the Marquis de Sade. Diane Arbus looked hard at freaks, searching maybe for a reservoir of innocence in this world. A few blocks east, at the Five Spot, Ornette Coleman eviscerated jazz essence through a raucous plastic sax. The great Charlie Mingus was also there, playing angular, complex, hard-driving music to a full house night after night. In salient forms of life and art, people exceeded themselves—or the self; our dashing President, John F. Kennedy, was screwing movie actresses. Everything dazzled.

Movies, the quintessence of excess, were becoming known as "films." To the reflective eye, Antonioni's movies were among the most important. Sylvia and I never missed one. We'd emerge radically deadened, yet exhilarated, sorry the movie had to end. She whispered once, as the lights came on, "Why can't they leave us alone?" It was truly painful, having to thrust back into the windy streets, back to our apartment. We carried away visions of despair and boredom, but also thrilling apprehensions of this moment, in this modern world, where emptiness could be exquisite, even a way of life, not only for Monica Vitti and Alain Delon but for us, too. Why not? Feelings were all that mattered, and they were available to us. We understood. We were susceptible to the ineffable strains and moods of modern life. We'd read Nietzsche. Our brainiest friends—not only sad little Agatha—brought regular news from the abyss. One of them, a graduate student in art history, was on heroin. Another, whose translations of Chinese poetry had won awards and a book contract, strolled the wall beside the Hudson River, a willing prey to rough trade.

I would come back to the apartment after shopping for groceries, or doing the laundry—Sylvia never did these things—and find Agatha lying about, telling all. I could hardly wait to hear it from Sylvia, stories about the wilderness of Manhattan where Agatha descended nightly. When she stayed very late, I'd walk her down into the street, then wait with her for a cab. I worried about her. She might run into trouble—hapless, defenseless girl—alone in the dark. I refused to acknowledge that she was excited by dangers of the unknown, running after trouble in the dark.

"It's too cold to wait out here," she said.

"No bother. I want to do it."

I peered down the avenue, freezing, praying for a cab to appear and take Agatha away. Then I hurried back to Sylvia. Agatha had told Sylvia how a boy forced her into prostitution. He took her to a boat docked on the West Side, then down into a small room. He kept her there until the men came, bestial types. While one did things to her, others watched. I imagined a steel room in the bottom of the boat, echoing with animal noises.

Repeating it to me—the boat, the small room, the men—Sylvia was ironically amused, posturing in her voice, mimicking Agatha's dull tones, as if to measure the distance between Agatha's lust for degrading experience and herself. I listened, feeling entertained without feeling guilty. I let myself imagine that Agatha was far gone, beyond recall, object more than subject, without claims on my humanity. I owed only politeness. A few minutes in the street waiting for a cab. What sympathy I felt was easy. Liking her was also easy. Affectations, corrosive cosmetics, stylish clothes, an aura of self-destructive debauch—she was utterly harmless, even sort of cute. I liked myself for liking her. She reported every peculiarity of her soul to Sylvia, but I didn't see, beneath Sylvia's contempt in retelling the stories, that she was involved in Agatha's fate. Then, one night in bed, Sylvia said, "Call me whore, slut, cunt . . ."

I was eventually to call her my wife. The old-fashioned name would make our life proper, okay. Things would change, I believed, though our fights had become so ugly that the gay couple across the hall wouldn't ever say hello to us. We passed frequently, almost touching, along the dingy route to the hall toilets, one dank closet for each apartment. They turned up their phonograph until it boomed above our shrieking. Eighteenth-century pieces, wildly flourishing strings and an extravaganza of golden trumpets, as if to remind us of high, vigorous civilization, where even the most destructive passions are sublimed. They hoped to drown us, maybe shame us, into silence. It never happened.

It's possible we frightened them with our horrendous daily battles, but I assumed they just didn't like us. They were repressed Midwestern types. Towheaded, hyperclean, quiet kids in flight from a small town, hiding in New York so they could be lovers, never supposing that their neighbors, just across the hall, would be maniacs. It struck me as paradoxical that being gay didn't mean you couldn't be disapproving and intolerant. I liked eighteenth-century music. Couldn't they tell? Forgive a little? Were their domestic dealings, because they behaved better, so different from ours? Sharing a bed, were they never deranged by sexual theatrics or loony compulsions? They passed us with rigid, wraithlike, blind faces. No hello, no little nod, only the sound of old linoleum crackling beneath us. They pressed toward the wall so as not to touch us inadvertently. We were an order of life beneath recognition. Their soaring music damned us. Their silence and their music threw me back on myself, made me think Sylvia and I—not the gay kids—were marginal creatures, morally offensive, in very bad taste. We were, but they seemed unjust. They really didn't know. I didn't either as I held

Sylvia in my arms and called her names and said that I loved her. Didn't know we were lost.

I have no job, no job, no job. I'm not published. I have nothing to say. I'm married to a madwoman.

(Journal, January 1962)

Soon after we were married, Sylvia said, "I have girlfriends who make a hundred dollars a week," which was a good salary in the early sixties. It would have paid two months' rent and our electric bills. But Sylvia meant, compared to her girlfriends, I was a bum. Eventually, I published a story or two in literary magazines, which made me happy, but the magazines paid nearly nothing. So I began looking for a job and, to my surprise, I was hired almost immediately as an assistant professor of English at Paterson State College in New Jersey. Then I stopped writing. I had much less time for stories, but more important was the fact that I was married. It changed my idea of myself. As a married man, I had to work for a living. I'd never believed writing stories was work. It was merely hard. The sound of my typewriter, hour after hour, caused Sylvia pain, and this was another reason to stop. But then whatever had importantly to do with me—family, friends, writing—shoved her to the margins of my consciousness, and she'd feel neglected and insulted.

This also happened if I stayed in the hall toilet too long, and it happened sometimes when we walked in the street. I'd be talking about a friend or a magazine article, maybe laughing, and I'd suppose that I was entertaining her, but then I'd notice she wasn't beside me. I'd look back. There she was, twenty feet behind me, down the street, standing still, staring after me with rage. "You make me feel like a whore," she said. "Don't you dare walk ahead of me in the street." Then she walked past me and I trailed her home, very annoyed, but also wondering if there wasn't in fact something wrong with my personality—talking, laughing, and having a good time, as if, like a moron or a dog, I was happy enough merely being alive. At the door to our building, Sylvia waited for me to arrive and open it for her, so that she could feel I was treating her properly, like a lady, not a whore.

She'd never say, "You're walking too fast. Please slow down." She'd slow down, lag behind, let me discover that I was treating her like a whore. And then it was too late. I'd done it, proved for the ten-thousandth time that I was bad. It was hard, from moment to moment—walking, talking, laughing, writing, shitting—not to say or do something that hurt Sylvia.

It was a nice day. I felt only a little miserable. I was going out to buy a winter coat. I was at the door when, suddenly, Sylvia wanted to make love, and she persisted endearingly. I didn't want to do it, and I didn't know how to say I didn't. Only Sylvia has that privilege. It became late afternoon, too late to go buy a coat. Sat in my room. I don't deserve a winter coat.

(Journal, January 1962)

The one time I got sick, I wanted only to go to sleep. I felt an apologetic reflex. If I went to sleep, Sylvia would feel abandoned. Still, I had to go to bed; sleep. I had a fever. I ached all over. It was only a cold, no big deal. But really, I had to lie down and sleep. The moment I shut my eyes, Sylvia began to sweep the floor around the bed. She decided I couldn't be allowed to lie there, sick, surrounded by a filthy floor, though we had roaches, fleas, and sometimes rats in the apartment, and there were holes in the walls through which spilled brown, hairy, fibrous insulation. She swept with great force. Then she washed the dishes, making a racket. Everything had to be cleaned because I was sick. She put clothes away in drawers, slamming them shut to make clear that order was being established, and she hustled about picking things up, straightening the place. When the apartment was as clean and orderly as she could make it, she said I couldn't lie on those sheets. We'd slept on them for several weeks. They were stained and dirty. I got out of bed and stood in my underwear, hot and shivering, while she changed the sheets. When she finished, I flopped back into bed. I fell asleep, but was soon awakened by an unnatural silence. I saw Sylvia standing at the foot of the bed, staring at me, shifting her weight from side to side as if she had to pee, looking frightened.

"You have to see a doctor," she said. "Get up. Get up."

"I come from peasant stock. Nothing can kill me."

"That isn't funny. Get up."

There was desperate urgency in her voice. I was too sick to argue with her. I got up and put on my clothes. We walked downstairs and then eight or nine blocks through the freezing night to the emergency room at St. Vincent's, then waited in line with drug addicts and crazies. Eventually, I was seen by a doctor. He said I had a cold. I should go to bed. Two or three hours after I'd gone to bed, I went to bed. Sylvia felt much better. In the morning, I was well.

She began a conversation about infidelity. How would I feel if she were unfaithful? I said we'd be through. She said, "Why, if it's just a mad moment brought on by general malaise?" I said, "Through. That's all." She said, "What if you didn't know?" I said, "If I didn't know, it's the same as if it never happened." She became increasingly angry, insisting that I accept her infidelity. "What if we're married ten years from now and have three kids, and we're at a party and both of us are unfaithful?" I said, "That's different. We'd be dedicated to the kids." She said, "You're not dedicated to anyone but yourself."

(Journal, January 1962)

During the week, I rose at 5:30 a.m. and rode the subway to the Port Authority Bus Terminal, then took a bus to Paterson, then another to the college, where I struggled up a steep hill, icy in the winter, to the office I shared with everyone in the English department. I taught classes morning and afternoon, had conferences with students, and then, as the sky darkened above the New Jersey landscape, made the long trip back to MacDougal Street, where I found Sylvia waiting for me. She was in good spirits when she did well at school, and once was very happy. She'd been given a small scholarship. Another time, I found her sprawled in a chair, shining with perspiration. Drawers had been emptied, contents strewn about the apartment. The bed was overturned. I stood in the living room, looking at her, and I tried to understand what had happened. I was still carrying my briefcase and wearing my coat. She studied my face, an ironic light in her eyes, as if she were seeing through me.

"All right," she said, "where is it?"

"Where is what?"

She laughed, tipping her head back arrogantly, as if to say I couldn't fool her with my innocent-sounding question.

"What's her name?"

I slowly realized she'd been searching the apartment for evidence of my infidelity—love notes, nude photos of my girlfriends, etc. There was no such evidence. There were only my journals, worse than love notes, but Sylvia never found them. We had an argument that lasted until long after midnight. My crime, real only in her head, couldn't be proved or disproved.

Bundled up and sweating in a heavy winter coat, my galoshes splashing in the sooty gray suck of New York snow, I lumbered down the empty, pre-dawn darkness of MacDougal Street toward the subway. My briefcase, fat with books and papers, bumped the side of my leg. At that hour, I'd see the big garbage truck from the city's sanitation department, men emptying pails into its loud, churning maw. There was no other sound. Nothing else moved in the street except me. It was an ugly way to greet the morning, but I liked my loneliness, and I liked getting out of the apartment. By the time I walked into the bus terminal, I felt rather good. My heart beat with a sense of purpose. My head was clear, untroubled by psychological complications. For the next eight hours, there would be no thoughts of Sylvia, and I'd feel no guilt for not thinking of her. I was hot and sweaty in my heavy coat, lumbering with the heavy briefcase through the terminal.

There was always a crowd of hats and coats, men packed together at the steamy breakfast counter where other men sliced oranges, smearing the halves down onto the spinning nozzle of a juicer. They moved with speed and grace. The steam carried good smells—hot coffee, cigarette smoke, baked dough and doughnut sugars. Standing in the crowd of silent men, I hunched over my orange juice, careful not to spill it, the taste bright as its color; or I'd sip hot black coffee, cup in one hand, cigarette in the other. Nervous oppression lay in most faces. They had lived like this for years. For me, charged up on caffeine and nicotine, it was new and real, the hustle and crush of city action, the New

York essence of it, the man's place. Wallowing in my clumsy galoshes, smoking the first cigarette of my day, I joined the solemn brotherhood of workers. I was happy.

I wasn't fucking my students, but I couldn't not look at them, couldn't not see that some of the Italian girls, from towns in

This is the man in Sylvia's life.
it could be her father,
it could be her brother,
it could be her husband.
It doesn't matter.
He can't even tell whether
he's coming or going.
Can you?

New Jersey, were visually delicious. At night, surrendering to fatigue, letting go of another day, I exuded what had been repressed in the classroom, like radioactive emissions of elemental decay. Memories came to me of the girls from Secaucus, Trenton, Paterson, and Jersey City, gorgeous girls with olive skin and lustrous, wavy hair. I never touched any of them. They had the handwriting of little children and drew bubbles over the letter *i*.

I thought of a million reasons not to touch. I wanted to touch. I didn't even flirt. I went home. I had sex only with Sylvia, me coming without much pleasure, she without coming. Our electrical frenzy—contortions, convulsions, thrashing, vicious kissing—left us wiped out and horny, needing something other, something more. I told myself I didn't need it, it wasn't important, though I looked at women in the subways and streets and my body said otherwise. I wasn't looking for a woman who would console me, or even a woman to whom I could talk without inciting violence. My body lusted. This was my secret infidelity, never confessed to my journals. Despite the daily misery of marriage, I wrote that I loved Sylvia. I wrote it repeatedly into my journals, and I wiped sincerely pathetic tears from my eyes. "I love Sylvia."

But to my shame, my body burned for the black woman in high heels and a tweed suit who stood near me while waiting for the D train at the West Fourth Street station. Not another person anywhere on the platform. She stood nearer than she had to. Sexual excitement hit suddenly, left me breathless. Did she want me to start a conversation? I'd never known anything like this. Marriage to Sylvia introduced me to a terrifying imperative: I needed another woman. I couldn't have said a word to this woman without seeming criminally deranged. There was also the woman who drove by in a silver Porsche at the corner of West Fourth and MacDougal. The car stopped for an instant in front of me. She gave me a deep look. It said our life together was about to begin if I seized the moment. Only to step forward, open the door, slide inside. She would drive me far away from here. We would never come back. And there was a young Puerto Rican mother carrying a shopping bag, who looked so weary and so beautifully appealing in the goodness of her dedication, her sacrifice. I felt love. I wanted to fuck her. She had magnificent lips and large green eyes. Instantly, these women were imprinted in my nerves and bones. I never said anything to them, never saw them again. I remembered them with love and despair. I began to remember them even before they were out of sight, as if they had never been more than memories, figures of a happier, former life.

Sylvia appears in my room. "I can't stand your typing."

"I'll be as quiet as possible."

"It doesn't matter. You exist."

She assumed a haughty posture, lit one of my cigarettes, flicked ashes on the floor. I felt a spasm of hate, but showed nothing. She didn't leave. I started to yawn. She pushed my jaw shut. I yelled. She looked concerned, then became angry, sneering at me. I was in pain. She could see it. She began wailing about all she had had to bear in the past year and a half.

I was in pain. She was wailing.

(Journal, January 1962)

In the spring of 1963 Sylvia completed her undergraduate work at NYU. We moved uptown to an apartment on West 104th Street, between West End Avenue and Riverside Drive. She took night classes in German. I continued teaching at Paterson State and joined a car pool. It made the trip easier. I came home less exhausted, and could go to a movie with Sylvia and not fall asleep in the middle of it. One of the drivers in the car pool, Dan Slater, was completing his graduate work at Columbia, writing a dissertation on French theater. He was gay. Mornings when he drove and there were no other riders, he'd talk about his latest lover, telling me what he liked about him, how long it would last, what the guy looked like, what he said. He talked about things I'd never heard mentioned before. He told me his feelings about some guy's cock. I was often shocked, but wouldn't show it. I told him, in a lighthearted, lying style, about the silly fight I'd had with Sylvia last evening. I didn't say we'd fought until 5 a.m., or that I'd had only an hour's sleep. I never talked about my life the way he talked about his, as if I were strangely embarrassed by the conventional limitations of marriage. One of his lovers, said Dan, thought the look of black metal wire twisted across front teeth was sexy. He asked Dan to find a dentist who would do the work. Dan didn't need braces. It would be expensive and painful, not to mention degrading.

"I said I won't do it. There was really nothing more to discuss."

"Who would do it?"

He laughed. "There are people who would."

"There are?"

"Oh, come on."

After a while, I was trying to write again. Another story was accepted by a literary magazine. I had also acquired a literary agent who became a good friend and visited us when we lived on MacDougal Street. One night he dragged me out to meet another writer represented by the agency. It was Jack Kerouac. I'd never spent an evening with a celebrity, but I had university friends who considered themselves intimates of Plato, Shakespeare, Marx, Freud, et al. Days later I asked one of them if he'd read Kerouac. He said, "Give me a break. I haven't read Proust yet."

In my agent's Porsche convertible, with the top down, we circled Manhattan, Kerouac raving about reviews of his books to the night sky. He'd memorized the cruelest comments, none funny, but he wanted us to laugh. We laughed. The night ended in a seedy bar near Fourteenth Street and Second Avenue. The floor was made of tiny, hexagonal, white-and-black tiles. There were booths of dark brown wood along one wall. Allen Ginsberg was there with some friends. Kerouac introduced us. I'd been introduced to Ginsberg a few times before, in Berkeley, but he never remembered me. It was like meeting on the great wheel of existence, going on to other lives, then meeting again, and not remembering we'd met before. Except I remembered.

When we moved uptown, we collected a new group of friends. Some of them taught at Columbia University, about ten short blocks north of our apartment. They often came by late at night, and we would sit talking and smoking marijuana until dawn. Our conversations, usually about literature or movies, were much influenced by marijuana, hence thrilling, but also very boring. As in Antonioni's movies, there was strange gratification in the boredom of our long, smoky, moribund-hip, analytical nights. Most of the time Sylvia was the only woman in the room. She'd pull her legs up on the couch and half lie there, looking sensuously langorous, yet very attentive to whatever the Columbia friends wanted to talk about, but then, pretty soon, she'd begin to disintegrate, becoming helpless with marijuana giggles, laughing at herself for laughing so much, and the Columbia friends would be tickled and they would laugh with her, encouraging her too much, I thought. But they had nothing at stake. Sylvia's susceptibility to marijuana was amusing, even endearing, to everyone except me. I feared and resented these moments, and I despised dope.

I never bought any dope, but it was often in the apartment. Friends "laid it on us," joints and pills, in return for our hospitality. They frequently showed up at our MacDougal Street apartment only to chat for a moment and get high before going on to some appointment in the neighborhood. Once, returning from the grocery store with a bag of food pressed to my chest, I passed an acquaintance who, saying hello, dropped three hashish cubes into the bag and went on. He'd never even visited the apartment, but dopers proselytized and were ordinarily very generous. Even the poorest of our drug friends would give part of whatever they had, as if with a religious spirit. They wanted you to get high with them, to feel the goodness they felt, and to see the world as they did. (Generosity stopped short of hard, expensive drugs.) The spirit of giving and religious community was good, I thought. Nothing like it had been seen before in the continuously murderous history of our country. But I'd put the joints and pills in a drawer, and forget about them until weeks later, when I came upon the stuff by accident and threw it out.

It never seemed to me, in the long hours of our marijuana nights, that Sylvia wasn't having a good time, even when there was only gasping and hissing in the room, as three or four of us sat with nothing to say, passing a joint around. She always seemed very content, and she was interested when conversation resumed. She always smoked, and she swallowed whatever pill was offered. A drawing she made gives an impression of our evenings. It shows Agatha, two of the Columbia friends, and an old friend of mine who stopped visiting after Sylvia and I got married. He is swooping in behind Sylvia with a knife, about to stab her in the back. The Columbia friends are stoned. I'm also in the drawing, typing, indifferent to everything happening in the room.

I was never indifferent, but I was trying to write, always trying again. That bothered Sylvia. Not the sound of my typing. I spent far more time with her than with the typewriter. What bothered her was that I wanted to do it. It was like going away, abandoning her. She'd listen patiently when I read my stories to her, and sometimes she liked them. She'd smile and say, "Yes." Her one word was tremendously pleasing. She could also be pretty hard. Once, after I read her a story, she said, "I still believe our child will be very intelligent."

The long conversational nights were also full of academic gossip about the English department at Columbia. Roger Lvov, an assistant professor who visited two or three times a week, often told us what had happened only hours earlier:

"I walked past Trilling's office this morning. The door was open."

Roger pressed the remains of his roach, pinched between the prongs of a bobby pin, to the tip of the funnel he made with

Sylvia + the man are spending
an evening with their friends.
They all have a lot to say.
But not to each other.
The man is being an artist.
You can tell by the way that he is laughing.
Do you see the radio in the corner,
Color it turned on high.
Color all the people turned on high too.

his lips. We waited for him to suck and then go on talking. His pale eyelids drooped, his nostrils tensed and blanched, opening wide. He sucked in three short, hard drafts. Essence of marijuana gas shot through the reticulations of his bronchial network. His eyes were crimson and glistening. He continued:

"Trilling looked at me as I went by the door. He could see me."

"Did he say anything?" I asked.

Roger gazed at me. "What?"

The question left me annoyed at myself. It was too eager, too curious. Later Sylvia would say Roger was laughing at me. He was going to repeat my question up and down West End Avenue and Broadway. She'd say I'd humiliated myself.

I burned as I asked again, "Did Trilling say anything to you?"

"No."

"Wow," said Theodore Edelweiss, whom we called Teddy, also an assistant professor at Columbia. He was more stoned than Roger and he seemed to believe that he had just heard a fantastic story. But I was not sure what Teddy thought. He was a complicated person, and might have been laughing at Roger.

Our Columbia friends knew they were going to be fired. It was the department's tradition to fire almost everyone, but no one could be absolutely sure if it would happen to him. Over the years, a few assistant professors had survived. To determine why anyone in particular survived was impossible. There was a story about an assistant professor who, upon being fired, became enraged and shouted at the chairman, "What do you want? Ten books? I'll write ten books. Twenty books? I'll write twenty books." Our friends didn't expect to survive, but didn't stop imagining they might. None of them published anything. Eventually, one by one, they lay before their senior colleagues who, like ancient Mayan priests, cut out their hearts. To their credit, they tried to destroy themselves first with drugs.

I was afraid that marijuana would intensify Sylvia's paranoia, and I pleaded with her not to smoke it unless I was there with her in the room. She would hide cigarettes and pills that came to her when I wasn't around. A few times she confessed that she'd smoked while I was in New Jersey or visiting my parents. I became outraged, I made puritanical scenes, but I wasn't consistent. If she took pills, I did, too. It was a way of being close, and as everyone knows, dope makes sex dreamy and long, when it doesn't just kill desire. We spent a three-day weekend in the apartment, eating speed, smoking grass, and reading and rereading *The Turn of the Screw*, for the evil feeling in this gruesome masterpiece. We ate no meals, didn't answer the phone, and we had bouts of hard, compulsive sex, after which we lay there aching for more. Toward the end of the third day, Sylvia began saying, "Open the window," as if these three words made a marvelous little poem:

O-pen.
The win-dow.

I asked her to stop, but she repeated it about a thousand times, in singsong tones, before collapsing beside me in a stupor, and then she told me what *The Turn of the Screw* is really about. Not the excruciating pleasure, taken by Henry James, in the fairy-tale tradition of tortured children. Sylvia was going on and on, both of us overwhelmed by her luminous ravings.

"I'll tell you what it's really about. Oh, my god, it's so obvious."

"I think you're right. That is it. That's what it's about."

She was so terrifically brilliant we had to have sex immediately. Later, neither of us remembered what she had said, not one word.

Sylvia told me that Agatha thinks of herself as being emotionally mature because she suffers no guilt for sleeping with anyone, male or female, friend or stranger, or for having sex in public, as she does with her girlfriend from the madhouse. "The two of them fondle each other while getting laid by their respective partners. At the same time."

"Emotionally mature?"

"She thinks."

"Agatha is depraved. I think."

Sylvia said angrily, "Agatha wouldn't hurt a soul. She just can't refuse herself anything. If she sees a pair of shoes she likes, she buys four pair. Same with sex."

"She's also a terrible gossip," I said. "No more idea of privacy in her mind than between her legs."

Afterwards, I regretted talking that way. I like Agatha. Maybe I was jealous. Sylvia and Agatha need each other. Agatha wants to talk, Sylvia wants to listen. Agatha's confessions are probably less depraved and more pleasing to her than her life, and they have kept her close to Sylvia. They are close even in their looks—same height, same shape. I found them asleep together, on the living room couch, one black-haired girl, one blonde. The difference only showed how much they looked the same, two girls lying on the couch in late afternoon. They looked like words that rhyme.

(Journal, April 1963)

In the conversational style of the day, everything was always *about* something; or, to put it differently, everything was always *really about* something other than what it seemed to be about. A halo of implication shimmered *about* innocuous words, movies, faces, and events reported in the newspapers. The plays and sonnets of Shakespeare and the songs of Dylan were all equally *about* something. The murder of President Kennedy was, too. Nothing was fully resident in itself. Nothing was plain.

Stoned on grass or opium or bennies or downers, lying side by side in our narrow bed as streetlights came on, we'd follow their patterns on the walls and ceiling as we listened to late-night radio talk shows. Our favorite was Long John Nebel. One night a caller said, in a slow, ignorant drawl, "Long John, you have missed the whole boat." Naked in our drugged darkness, we turned to each other with a rush of sweet, gluey love and happiness. For months thereafter, we said affectionately, "You have missed the whole boat."

Sylvia could be happy and funny, but it is easier to remember the bad times. They were more sensational; also less painful now than remembering what I loved. There were moments when we'd happen to look up at each other while sitting a few yards apart in a crowded subway train, or across a room at a party, or in the slow flow of drugged conversation with four others in our living room, the gray dawn beginning to light the windows, and we'd smile with our eyes, as if we were embarrassed by our luck, having each other.

One afternoon, alone in the apartment, I found myself staring at Sylvia's sneaker lying on the floor beside the bed. It was still laced. She'd shoved it off her foot with the heel of the other sneaker, which was nowhere in sight. What came to me was the terrifying emptiness of the sneaker. I couldn't remain alone in the apartment. I left and walked quickly toward the Columbia campus, trying to spot her in the crowd, black hair flying, brown leather coat.

Roger phoned, then came by. He told me that he shot up last night, and had gone to sleep at eight in the morning. He was awakened by a phone call, at 9:45 a.m., from his aunt. Wretched with no sleep, he tried to be polite. While talking to his aunt, he noticed tiny bugs moving about his crotch. I imagined Roger sprawled in bed, talking on the phone, playing with himself, and suddenly noticing the local fauna. The aunt said, "I've got a girl for you."

Roger said, "Really?"

"She's blonde, works in television, and is charming. Promise me you'll call."

Roger said, "I promise."

After hanging up, Roger spent twenty minutes immobilized by horror and fascination, staring at tiny white bugs crawling on his skin.

Before he could tell me all this, Roger said I had to swear not to repeat a word of it. He always does something to make me wait before saying what he has in mind. He lights a cigarette, or stares into my eyes and says nothing. The effect is eerily suspenseful. Finally, whatever he says is anticlimactic. I swore I wouldn't tell anyone. He said:

"I think I have syphilis."

I asked why he thought so.

"A late stage of syphilis."

I asked again why he thought so.

"There are little animals crawling on me. I also have a rash."

I didn't laugh. I advised him to call a doctor. From my place he phoned his doctor friend, Jerry, Roger's roommate at Harvard. Jerry told Roger he probably didn't have syphilis, and he explained about pubic lice. Jerry phoned in a prescription to a nearby drugstore. Roger and I walked up Broadway together to pick it up. I wondered if it is remarkable that Roger Lvov, a genius from Brooklyn who has a Harvard Ph.D., thinks pubic lice indicate a late stage of syphilis.

(Journal, July 1963)

At the end of the school year, I resigned from my job at Paterson State, applied for readmission to graduate school at the University of Michigan, and began to audit classes at Columbia to recover the feeling of lectures and the formal study of literature. I also started reading again in a scholarly mood, with attention to style and meaning, and no pleasure. There were more fights with Sylvia. After a bad fight, when both of us were spent, I said quietly that I would leave New York. She said nothing. I took her silence as agreement.

One night, around 11 p.m., we were going to an all-night movie house on 42nd Street. As we descended into the subway, a rush of air, urinous and greasy, lifted about us. I said, "I can't go down there. Let's walk." Sylvia didn't mind walking. We'd gone only a few blocks when it began to drizzle. The sidewalk became slick. She tripped, soiled her white dress, and tore the strap of her sandal. I thought she'd blame me, but she didn't. She was ready to go on walking. I wasn't. I hailed a cab. As we were driving down Broadway, the cab rattling and clicking, the wide street shining on either side, I saw that in her soiled white dress, her black hair sparkling with rain, she was very pretty. I looked at her, memorizing the shape of her neck and mouth and the bones of her face, and I thought, She is my wife. I am leaving her.

Sometimes, after a fight, we went to the movies. It was like going to church. We entered with the people, found our seats, faced the light, and succumbed to the vast communal imagination. We came away feeling affectionate and good, wounds healed. In the all-night movies on 42nd Street, we'd sit in the balcony with the great smokers and popcorn people, their fingers scrabbling, mouths gnashing. Others sucked chocolate, licked ice cream, and rattled candy wrappers. There were drunks and half-wits who talked to the screen. Bums spit on the floor. This was honest-to-god-movies, place of Manhattan's sleepless people, like a zoo but in its massive anonymity, private-feeling. We could go to the movies together even though, twenty minutes earlier, we'd been screaming murder. In the silent desolation after a fight, I might say:

"You want to go to the movies?"

Sylvia would straighten her clothes, check her face in the bathroom mirror, grab her leather coat and tie the wraparound belt as we went out the door. I loved seeing her quickness, particularly in her hands, when she gave herself to something. We'd hurry off to the subway without finding out when the movie began, because there would always be two movies. We could watch at least one from the beginning.

Sitting in the balcony, the eating and smoking all around, I sank into creaturely happiness, and then I noticed my arm was around Sylvia's shoulder, and she had leaned her head on my arm. Our bad feelings were annihilated by big faces of love shining on the wall. Later, back in the street world, electricity lashed at our eyes, crowds mauled us, traffic wanted to kill us, and evil birds of marriage, black flecks soaring high in our brains, threatened to descend, but we were going home, we'd soon be in bed, hidden, pressed closely together.

A few years earlier, in 1959, I had stood in line to buy tickets outside the Guild, a movie house in Berkeley, owned by Pauline Kael. Her brief movie reviews, posted near the box office, were masterpieces of tone, often better than the movies. She made them feel crucially personal, like novels and poems. Walker Percy's novel, *The Moviegoer*, published in 1961, about the time Sylvia and I got married, said movies were personally redemptive; in the loneliness of an American life, moments of grace.

Teddy asked if I would do him a favor and listen to him read a chapter of his dissertation aloud. I told him I would come to his place this afternoon. Spending time with Teddy, without Sylvia present, felt awkward, as if I were betraying her. She'd be resentful. She likes Teddy. He's attractive and smart, and he flatters her with small attentions, laughing at her least joke.

She'd feel left out. Teddy read for almost an hour. It was a great pleasure. Two of us in a room thinking about literature as if nothing could be more serious. Teddy says when the ghost in *Hamlet* walks onto the stage, one kind of hero becomes another in tragedies of revenge. I wanted to applaud. In my excitement I blurted out, "The ghost is wearing armor, he's dressed for battle, but he can't do anything except talk and scare people. He's just like his son." Teddy looked as if I'd made him sick. I should have listened, and said his ideas are good, that's all. My enthusiasm had been wrong in spirit, a touch competitive. Before he finished, the phone rang. It was his ex-wife. She needed advice about an abortion for a relative. Teddy looked nervous after the call. He talked about his ex-wife's habit of jumping into the troubles of other people. Before saying goodbye, she asked Teddy what he was doing. He said he was writing his dissertation. She said, "You've found something to torture yourself with." Teddy said their conversations begin innocuously, then something gives her a chance to slash at him. I had ruined his mood, and then she knocked him off balance. He was confused, didn't know how to stop talking. He's the smoothest, drawing-room man in New York, but he'd embarrassed himself, showing me his distress, bad-mouthing his ex-wife. He said, "She's not like Sylvia, right?" The question was ironical, a thrust at me, but I didn't know what was intended. He is protected by fifty smooth surfaces; never has a feeling that isn't a little hidden. He didn't want to go on reading now, and smoked a whole joint by himself, forgetting to offer me a drag. I didn't want a drag, but I was uncomfortable not being offered one. It seemed more hostile than forgetful. He asked suddenly if I had seen the Rodin show.

"Yes."

"Great, isn't he?"

"I suppose. I always liked Degas's sculptures."

"I hate Degas."

I went home feeling sad. The cost of our friendship exceeded its value.

(Journal, August 1963)

In July 1963, shortly before I separated from Sylvia and went to Michigan, I scribbled a note in my journal: "Movie. Sylvia fled. I met Roger alone. No Rosalie." What happened was that Roger phoned and we made a date to meet in front of the Carnegie delicatessen, then go to a movie. Roger said he was bringing Rosalie. We'd heard about Rosalie for months, but never met her. This would be an exciting occasion. Roger told us the clever things Rosalie said about movies. But does Rosalie go to school? Does Rosalie have a job? Roger smiled in his weirdly embarrassed manner, repeating the words "school" and "job," and he looked arch, as if we'd said much more than we knew. It was his sort of game. He had a secret. We knew what he was being secret about, but, out of affection for Roger, we played along. Eventually, we stopped asking about Rosalie. We thought of her mainly as a mind who went to movies with Roger and made clever comments. She had no body. Roger, a bookish man, looked as if he'd never been introduced to his own body. He was skinny, with flat buttocks, broad Slavic face, thin lips, exceptionally pale complexion, gray eyes, and dark-blond hair combed straight back. His posture was stick-like, and he seemed to carry unusual pressure high up in his chest, like a drowning man, gasping for air before going under. His lips worked with thoughts, tasting words before he spoke them.

We took a bus downtown and got to the Carnegie delicatessen earlier than we expected, leaving us twenty minutes to wait, probably longer. Roger never arrived on time. Sylvia complained about the heat and was annoyed because I hadn't worn a tie. On this particular afternoon, not wearing a tie showed disrespect for her. It was too hot for a tie, but I didn't make that point. I was trying to be pleasant, not fight about anything. I was the one who was leaving town. Even with good reason to leave, the leaver is in the wrong. I'd have surely put on a tie, though it was unnecessary and uncomfortable, but Sylvia hadn't mentioned it until we were out in the street. I felt set up, frustrated, given no chance to be good and avoid trouble. Roger would be wearing a tie and jacket. Sylvia had him in mind, comparing him to me, his tie showing respect for Rosalie. Roger always had a formal air, like a boy whose mother once told him, "You should always wear a jacket and tie." His trousers rode too high on his hips. Grease spots appeared on his shirt fronts, like a family crest. He mixed materials, heavy tweed jacket with shiny gabardine slacks. The effect was formal and tasteless, almost sleazy.

Outside the Carnegie delicatessen, I took my money out of my pocket to see if I had enough for tickets and dinner. I needed about ten dollars. Sylvia said, "You're not going to count your money in the street, I hope." After that, I had no choice but to count my money, but I didn't do it. I stuffed the bills back into my pocket. Irascible and silent, we waited for Roger and his Rosalie. The minutes in the afternoon heat stood like buildings along the avenue, utterly still. Sylvia asked me to feel her lower back. I put my hand there. Her blouse was damp with sweat. I said, "Mm. Yeah." My tone was sympathetic. Then she asked for money to buy a can of talcum powder. She wanted to shake talcum powder into her shoes in front of the Carnegie delicatessen. I gave her all my change, about thirty-five cents. It must have seemed to her enough for only one can of talcum powder, which cost about twenty cents. I had not brought several million dollars with me for the tons of talcum powder she might need. She was visibly angry and spun away from me and hustled off to a drugstore. In a minute she returned without talcum powder, and said, "The drugstore is full of Scandinavian airline people." She meant she couldn't get service. "This ruins the evening. I can't possibly enjoy anything after this." She also meant tall blond gorgeous men and women.

I said, "Let's get coffee," and I started across the avenue toward a diner. Sylvia's hatred pushed me ahead of her, but I made myself go slow. We walked together for half a minute in silence. Then she said, "I'm going to Fifth Avenue. I'll take the bus home from there."

Without a word, I walked into the diner, sat at the counter. Sylvia watched me through the plate glass window. When I looked at her, she frowned with dark hurt angry disbelief, then walked away. A surging weight, like a body within my body, lunged after her, running out of the diner and down the street to catch her, beg her not take the bus home, but stay, meet Roger and Rosalie, go to the movie. I didn't move. I'd begged too many times. Please come with me to visit my father in the hospital, please come with me to dinner at my parents' apartment, please come with me to the party, please let's go to the psychiatrist, please get out of bed. I ordered a hamburger. When it came, I bit into it once or twice, swallowed without chewing, and left the rest of it on the plate. I walked back to the Carnegie.

Roger was there in his jacket and tie, stick-like, pale as a vampire in the sunlight. He grinned, holding air in his rigid neck. I saw no Rosalie. I knew he wanted to ask, "Where's Sylvia?" But he was unsure if he could. Unbearable revelations might follow. Better not to ask. Think. Suspect. Sniff about for clues. Analyze. I was irritated at him for being like himself.

What I'd found endearing other times was suddenly contemptible. I didn't explain Sylvia's absence. Too ashamed. "Where's
Rosalie?" I asked. Roger muttered about a migraine headache.
I didn't believe Rosalie had a migraine headache. I knew damn
well Rosalie was a man. Roger had decided once again that a Jewish boy from Brooklyn does not come out. We went to the movie,
This Sporting Life, together. At one point the hero says, "I can
love, can't I?" Movies often asked that depressing question.

I told Sylvia I would see a psychiatrist when we separated. She
said it wouldn't do any good because I couldn't remember facts.
I'd give a distorted account of our marriage. Then we talked
about her girlfriend Betty whose boyfriend, Matthew, is very
loving. "He took her skin diving in Puerto Rico."

"Do you want to go skin diving in Puerto Rico?"

"That's not the point."

Sylvia said Matthew doesn't worry about Betty not being
good-looking enough for him. I said, "I don't worry either.
You're a fanatic on the subject of looks." She rolled away. Then
she turned and said, "You didn't think I was a fanatic when I
was your little jewel." There were tears in her eyes. She rolled
away again and asked me to shut off the light. I did, then went
into the bathroom and picked at my face, making it bleed. When
I crawled back into bed, she said, "Agatha's parents have been
divorced and married twice—to each other." I said, "There are

no happy marriages." She said, "What about your parents?" I said, "They live in another world."

(Journal, August 1963)

The train from Grand Central to Ann Arbor, Michigan, was called the Wolverine. The trip took ten hours, from dark to dawn. In the long clattering night, hungry, unable to sleep, I opened the paper bag of sandwiches, cookies, and coffee Sylvia prepared for me. She had never done anything like that before. Now that we were separating, I'd been unable to stop her. When I unscrewed the aluminum cap of the thermos bottle, a small folded paper fell out. I opened it and read a penciled note from Sylvia: *I love you.*

She loves me, I thought, and nothing more, as night hurtled by the window, a black animal pierced by the tiny lights of houses in the distant countryside. I ate everything in the bag and drank the coffee. I smoked until I felt only the heat and tear of cigarette devastations.

A few weeks passed before Sylvia decided to join me in Michigan. Her decision was impulsive and sentimental. I didn't object. I missed her. I never looked at my journals and I remembered none of the small, mean daily miseries that were the texture of our life in New York. I might have remembered if I tried, but I didn't try. I didn't think. I was a little anxious, but mainly very happy to see her when she got off the train, her black bangs and bright black eyes. As she came toward me, she smiled broadly and walked with a rocking motion, like a fat little kid, showing me how full of goodness she felt, as if she'd just eaten a big meal. Proud and silly at once, showing her happiness.

Our fights began again in Michigan and were as bad as those in New York. One night she stood at the bathroom mirror and methodically smashed at her reflection with a metal ashtray, the glass streaking and flashing out of the frame. She said:

"You (*smash*) don't (*smash*) love (*smash*) me (*smash*). But you will miss me."

I helped her pack and I took her to the train station. Though very anxious, we didn't fight. We were, instead, melancholy and affectionate. This was it. The end. She was wearing a plain black cocktail dress, hemmed slightly above the knee. She looked very sophisticated and pretty. I kissed her on the lips. She didn't quite kiss me back. She returned to New York, and then I was wretched in a whole new way, because I wasn't really wretched and I felt guilty about it. I wrote to her and phoned her frequently. It was over and yet we persisted, though a bit less and a bit less as the weeks went by. My letters were playful and affectionate. On visits to New York during school vacations, I stayed with my parents, or occasionally with Sylvia in her new apartment on Sullivan Street. Like the one on MacDougal Street, it was hardly more than a room. We made love again, in our manner, as if we believed we could make real whatever it was that bound us to each other. Before my last visit, Christmas vacation, 1964, Sylvia returned to the apartment near Columbia, which she had sublet while living on Sullivan Street. I went to New York with the intention of talking to her about a divorce. We'd never mentioned divorce. I didn't know how to bring it up. I expected fury and violence, and I very much dreaded it.

I can't remember exactly how we first agreed to separate, only that there had been a fight and I said I was going to leave, go back to Michigan. Sylvia hadn't seemed distressed by the idea. I thought maybe she looked forward to being free and independent in Manhattan. The adventure of total availability. Then, a few weeks before I left for Michigan, she said very obliquely that other men would be interested in her. "I'm sure you'll have no trouble finding somebody when I'm gone," I answered. Instantly, she flew at me, tearing at my face. I swatted her hands away reflexively, with a sidewise motion, and must have brushed her nose or slapped her hands into her nose. I felt only her hands. I didn't feel any part of her face. She shrieked, "You broke my nose," and lunged at the living room window, tearing at the blinds and shrieking for the police. She mutilated the blinds but didn't manage to open the window, and she was still shrieking, "Police, police, help," as I dragged her away from the window and tried to hold her still and look at her nose. She pushed me back and dashed into the bathroom. Leaning over the sink, she stared closely at her face in the mirror, saying, "It's broken. Look." It looked no different, and then it did look different. I couldn't tell.

I hadn't felt my hand touch her nose, but I apologized again and again, and I studied her nose carefully, respectfully, almost hoping to see that it was broken. In her mind she had a broken nose and I had broken it. There was no other way of looking at the situation, and nothing to think about. Her nose was broken. She stayed at the mirror a long time, slowly turning her face this way and that, an excited glow in her eyes, like an artist studying a piece of work with quiet satisfaction.

Finally, in a mood of strained reconciliation, we went out to find a doctor. Our apartment was only a block from West End Avenue, where the ground floor of many buildings was given over to the offices of doctors, dentists, and psychiatrists. Like a great medical center, every specialty was available to the thousands who lived in the buildings. We picked a name and rang the bell. The doctor himself answered and agreed to look at Sylvia's nose right then. It was late afternoon. There happened to be no patients in his waiting room. His nurse and receptionist had gone home. He had wispy gray hair, brown philosophical eyes, and a middle-European accent. He touched Sylvia's nose, pressing lightly on one side, then the other. Glancing at me, he said with mock dismay, "He didn't do it, did he?"

Sylvia said, "No. He's too kind."

They sounded as if they were related, both of them mildly witty and ironical. The doctor said he didn't think her nose was "fractured," let alone broken. I was pleased by his word, but I knew Sylvia wouldn't accept it. She asked if he would refer her to a specialist.

"What kind of specialist?"

"A plastic surgeon."

I then realized Sylvia wanted to believe she had a broken nose. Fixing it would be her excuse to shorten it. That evening Roger phoned and said, "I have a grotesque request. I need two hundred dollars." I said I could lend him fifty dollars. Sylvia overheard. Much annoyed, she said, "You have to pay for my operation." I'd leave for Michigan. She'd have a nose job.

The surgeon's office was on Park Avenue. Well-dressed women sat in his waiting room, one or two with bandaged noses. There were no magazines, only photo albums showing patients before and after plastic surgery, noses much shortened. There were no pictures of men. Nostril holes stood up and gaped like a second pair of eyes. I noticed that the surgeon's receptionist and two nurses had noses like the ones in the photos—Pekingese snouts—his mark, his vision. The women, it seemed, had wanted to please the surgeon. It was unimaginable that they'd pleased themselves. I thought to warn Sylvia against the doctor, but she hadn't yet decided to have surgery and it might have caused a dispute in the waiting room. I showed her one of the albums, turning pages without comment, letting her see what this doctor could do with a nose.

When one of the nurses called Sylvia, I went too. I was uncomfortable being there, but she wanted me along. I followed her through a room divided into half a dozen curtained stalls, where the surgeon saw post-operative patients, perhaps five or six an hour. He received us in his office, a big, thick-chested man with a mangled-looking, heavy Jewish face, a huge nose, and a voice that seemed to rumble at us through a sewer pipe.

Sylvia talked shyly about her broken nose, saying not a word about surgery. I supposed she had been shaken by the photo albums. As she talked, the surgeon stared at her nose. She was hesitant, smiling pitifully, and said only that she thought her nose might have been broken. It didn't look quite straight. Perhaps something could be done.

He told Sylvia to sit on a stool, then stood before her, cupped the back of her head with both hands, and pulled her face toward him, gradually mashing her nose against his belly, harder and harder, holding it there for about ten seconds. Then he released her. Sylvia was in great pain. The doctor wrote her a prescription for six sleeping pills, and said, in an offhand manner, her nose "could be shorter." His fee was a hundred dollars.

When we were back in the apartment, Sylvia took a ball-point pen and put a two before the six in the prescription. I was reluctant to take it to the drugstore. Why would a doctor prescribe twenty-six of anything? The druggist might phone the doctor to confirm the amount. Sylvia said there was nothing to worry about. I owed it to her, after breaking her nose, to take the risk. I went.

While I was waiting for the pills, a young man came in and asked for cigarettes. The druggist stopped working on my prescription, and went for the carton of cigarettes. Then the man asked to have them wrapped.

The druggist said, "What for? Is it a gift?"

The man said, "It's against the law to leave with a carton of cigarettes that is not wrapped."

I wanted the twenty-six pills. I wanted to get out of there.

The druggist said, "I never heard of such a law."

I realized that he was no less of a nut than his customer.

The man said, "If I walk out of this drugstore with a naked carton of cigarettes, people will think I stole it."

The druggist said, "I'll testify in your behalf."

I groaned. The druggist heard me. With an expression of disgust, he wrapped the carton of cigarettes.

I thought, This is New York. I will be leaving soon.

When the man walked away with his wrapped carton of cigarettes, the druggist said, "I'll drive him crazy before he drives me crazy." Then he gave me twenty-six sleeping pills. I hurried back to the apartment.

I'd merely said she would have no trouble finding somebody after I left, and the result was the "broken nose." To talk about a divorce might result in more destruction. But I had to talk about divorce. We'd been living separate lives for over a year.

I'd been seeing another woman. I didn't tell Sylvia about her. I didn't know if Sylvia was seeing other men. She intimated things on the telephone, but was always so vague that, without sounding jealous, I couldn't ask if she was telling me that she was fucking somebody. I didn't want to hear about it, anyway. She did the best she could, I suppose, to be honest. Neither of us had the courage to speak plainly.

In New York, near the end of my vacation, December 30, 1964, I went uptown from my parents' apartment to meet Sylvia. I was determined to talk about a divorce, and I was sure it would be the hardest thing I ever had to do.

I don't remember if I met Sylvia at the apartment or if we met in a restaurant, but we were in a restaurant late in the evening, and I was surprised to find another man present. Sylvia's friend. He was blond and French, a graduate student at Yale. He had a soft, sensuously handsome face and a heavily suggestive, ironic smile. It suggested he was amused by complexities that left other people baffled and in pain. I thought, This guy is an asshole, but if Sylvia likes him, I like him. Anyhow, Sylvia's friend was too beautiful, obviously a lover, nobody's friend. With him in the picture, talking about a divorce might be no problem. Sylvia might even bring it up herself. At some point in the evening, Sylvia said good-night to the Frenchman. I don't remember that he and I said good-night to each other, or that we had even

been introduced. He was just no longer at the table. I was surprised again, having expected Sylvia to say good-night to me,
not him. With him gone, Sylvia and I walked to the apartment.

The New Year's Eve celebration had begun early. There was
garbage and broken glass everywhere. Streets were splattered
with vomit, as if strewn with hideous bouquets of blazing col-
or. Things seemed nightmarish, but Sylvia and I were walking
home as we had many times, as if nothing essential had changed
between us. She'd surely been involved with the Frenchman,
but I didn't think about it. The naturalness of our being together this minute, made me wonder: Is this love? and, if you're
ever in love, does the feeling for that person go away? Sylvia
pressed my side and held my arm. I felt married to her forever,
and I assumed that she would expect me to spend the night,
and we would have sex. Whenever I came to the city, I spent
some nights with her. But I didn't want to spend the night. I
didn't want sex. I had to talk about divorce. The subject seemed
incongruous. The mood was all wrong. I felt no anger, no bitterness, only vague anxiety about the future. There was no feeling
in me that could usher the subject into words.

I told Sylvia that I would be taking my preliminary exams
in two weeks. She talked about her civil service job. At the apartment, she changed into a short gray cotton nightgown and
poured herself a glass of bourbon. She then joined me on the
living room couch, lying on her back with her head in my lap.
It wasn't the moment to talk about divorce, but if I talked about
anything else, it would be a lie. I was calm, listening to her,

waiting for my chance to mention the serious matter, the one real thing, and put an end to this comfortable, mechanical, unreal domestic intimacy. Even if, somehow, I loved her and would always love her, our life together was hell, and could never be otherwise. I told myself to remember this.

Sylvia talked easily, addressing the air above, not my face. I noticed a black cat in the apartment. It had a broken tail, shaped like a flattened Z, or a lightning bolt. I watched the cat and it watched me. It was wretched-looking, a cat that skulked about, as if it felt guilty of being unlikeable.

Sylvia told about men she'd been seeing in the past several months. Some were my friends. She let me know that she'd been sleeping with them by telling me little gossipy stories.

"Teddy found out I was seeing one of his colleagues. He was very jealous. He said, 'Now I know what Othello feels like.'"

Her tone was amused and blasé, as if none of this could be painful to me. She went on for a long time, quite comfortable reviewing her affairs while lying with her head in my lap. I listened without saying a word. Her French friend, I supposed, had been an object lesson, an introduction to what she planned to say when we were alone. She was mildly theatrical, stopping occasionally to lift her head and take another sip of bourbon. When the glass was empty, she refilled it, then went on about this one and that one. She'd even slept with Roger, who was still trying to decide whether he preferred men. They'd taken drugs together. One night Roger and Teddy were both in the apartment. They each knew the other was sleeping with Sylvia.

There was awful tension in the room. Everyone smoked a lot of grass, and, for hours, they talked about sexual perversion in Shakespeare's sonnets. Neither Roger nor Teddy would leave before the other. Then, around 3 a.m., Roger went to the bathroom. The moment he left the room, Teddy pushed Roger's chair all the way to the kitchen door, almost out of the living room. When Roger returned he saw the empty space and, of course, being himself, he was baffled. He suspected something had changed, but he wasn't sure. He certainly wouldn't ask. Then he saw his chair near the kitchen door. He went to it and sat there the rest of the night while Teddy and Sylvia sat in the living room in a normal way, and nobody said anything about what had happened. Sylvia laughed a little as she told the story, still feeling flattered by the idea of her two highly intellectual lovers. She also mentioned an editor of gourmet cookbooks who, even in literary circles of Manhattan where there is no shortage of satyrs, was notorious. I knew the guy. I hadn't seen him in years, but we had friends in common and I heard plenty about him. He was a pretty man with curly brown hair, curly mouth, angelic blue eyes, rosy cheeks, and a soft lyrical voice. He had the grand style of a courtly, sentimental seducer. He read poems and sang songs to women. Several thousand women had been laid in his midtown apartment. I'd heard that the full-length mirror inside his closet door reflected the bed, but you couldn't see the reflection from the bed unless you knew where to look. It was cast down the hall to another mirror inside a hall closet door. In bed with the woman of the moment, he could watch her in the hall closet mirror. He'd turn her this way and that, and she wouldn't know she was being watched. The idea of self-conscious Sylvia subjected to his mirrors was sad.

About an hour passed with me locked in my old psychological prison, wondering if I'd ever feel good again. She'd given me plenty of reason to bring up divorce, to say simply that I wanted a divorce, but she was doing all the talking, sipping her bourbon, gaily confessing her infidelities. I might have said that I was seeing somebody, too, but it was only one person and she seemed irrelevant. I had nothing very dramatic, or interesting, to say about her. She didn't even smoke, let alone take drugs. The moment belonged to Sylvia. I could say nothing at all. Then she asked, "Would you like to try once more?" She meant resume our life in Michigan, while I completed work for the Ph.D. The question was stupefying. I hadn't expected anything like that, but maybe I should have known it was coming.

At the moment, I didn't try to figure things out. I could repeat every word she said, but I understood little, maybe nothing. She seemed a different person, no longer the shy, pathologically sensitive, explosive Sylvia, the one who was attractive to men yet felt she was repulsive. This was a glamorous Sylvia, an intellectual's whore, sipping bourbon and flaunting her adventures in love, then asking if I'd like to have her back, as if she'd proved herself ravishingly depraved, brilliant in destructive spirit, perversely irresistible. I sat bloated by misery, heavy, stupid, burning. She'd said enough. She waited for my answer.

"Wait till I finish my exams," I said. "Then come to Ann Arbor."

She heard me. I said it clearly. I never felt worse. Sylvia lay still for a while, weighing my words. Then she sat up and walked into the bedroom. I continued to sit on the couch, unable to talk, a dummy. She reappeared, stood at the end of the couch, and said, "I just swallowed forty-seven Seconals." In her eyes, I saw a flat look of that's that, and there you have it.

I said, "You're kidding."

She walked off to the bathroom. I stayed where I was, on the couch, not believing her, not disbelieving, and then I heard her groan. Her body fell to the floor, which is how it sounds. It does not sound like anything else. I hurried to the bathroom. She was sprawled on the tile, underpants still hooked to one ankle. Apparently she'd fallen off the bowl while sitting on it. I dragged her to the couch, shouting at her, slapping her face, shaking her. Then I tried to walk her around the living room. I stopped only to phone the police, and open the apartment door wide, and then I went back to the bathroom, picked up her underpants, and pulled them up her legs. I tried again to make her walk, hooking her left arm around my shoulder, my right arm about her waist. It was no use. I was dragging her, not walking her. I dropped her back on the couch, straddled her, and pleaded and shouted while shaking her and furiously rubbing her wrists. I thought to make her vomit, but she was unconscious and I was afraid she would choke. Minutes later, two policemen entered the apartment. They did the same thing with Sylvia that I'd been doing, one on either side of her, walking her about. Then there was an ambulance, lights flashing in the street. We carried Sylvia downstairs. I got into the ambulance with her. We shot across town to Knickerbocker Hospital, in Spanish Harlem.

A medical team was waiting to receive Sylvia. They went to work in an efficient, military way. I saw them cup her mouth with a respirator mask, then somebody asked me and the two policemen not to stand so close. We retreated to the doorway. As if I weren't there, one policeman said to the other, "She won't make it."

It had been less than half an hour since she fell. She was healthy; only twenty-four years old. It was impossible that she could just die, regardless of the liquor and the pills; but there she was, unconscious and responding to nothing. I was scared. I thought only in the most primitive manner. She'd always been right about everything. I'd always been wrong. I loved her. I couldn't live without her. She'd proved it. I was convinced. No more proof was necessary, only that she open her eyes and live. I'd be what she liked. I'd do what she wanted and that would also be what I wanted. She would know that I loved her and always had. My mind went round and round with the same little prayer. I had only to keep saying it, not let any other thought interfere. It was important not to be distracted. In this trancelike state, I could see other people all about and I could converse, and yet I was isolated, I was pure, dedicated to my prayer, as if it were keeping Sylvia alive. I loved her, I had always loved her, we were going to Michigan . . .

One of the medical staff asked me if I knew what Sylvia had swallowed. I told him what she said. He then said they must do a tracheotomy. Sylvia wasn't breathing. But no one present had authority to perform a surgical procedure. I noticed that all of them had foreign accents, Spanish and German. Perhaps they weren't fully licensed to practice medicine in America. They were standing around, suddenly doing nothing. I didn't understand how there could be nothing to do. I urged the one who spoke to me to do the tracheotomy. I said, "Please do it." I begged with my face and body and voice. He wanted to do it, but was frightened. Another doctor appeared, wearing street clothes, coming down the hall, walking briskly to the exit. He was a tall, strong-boned man with a Nordic face, sallow complexion, thin lips, icy eyes. He looked authoritative, like a hero or a god, one who could perform surgery, climb a mountain, kill people, anything. I saw in his eyes that he was thinking only of leaving the emergency room, going away from this hospital, going to a place far away. The one who'd spoken to me, a short dark Spanish doctor—if he was a doctor—stopped the one who was leaving. He explained the situation to him in an deferential tone; a slight bend appeared in his spine and his elbows pressed his ribs, as if he were making the shape of apology, begging forgiveness. With a gesture of disgust, the tall one brushed him aside and went out the door.

I'd known instantly that the Spanish doctor had used the wrong tone. He should have been assertive and demanding. He should have said in a loud voice for everyone to hear, "Do it. She isn't breathing. She'll die." Instead, he was a whispering, servile man. I'd been afraid the doctor with icy eyes would react just as he did, brushing the Spanish doctor aside. I could do nothing except watch the two men, as if I were dreaming their entire exchange.

The Spanish doctor then returned to Sylvia. The others stood about the table, grimly watching as he performed the tracheotomy. I watched from the doorway, forbidden to step closer. The Spanish doctor was taking a chance with his career and his life. At least that's what I thought. With everything to lose, he did the job.

Moments later he turned to me and said Sylvia would be all right. She was breathing normally. He was pleased, exultant, reassuring; his successful performance had left us nothing to worry about. They wheeled her away to a room upstairs. I followed and sat beside her bed. When we were alone, I told her we would go to Michigan, and that I wished she would open her eyes. She didn't open her eyes, didn't move.

I left the room to phone family and friends. Some arrived in the middle of the night, others early the next morning. Two of Sylvia's aunts and an uncle were among those who came. They spoke to one another, not to me. I overheard a few things they said while they stood talking outside Sylvia's room.

"I feel terrible. I never visited her. She would call me sometimes." It was a woman's voice, matronly, with a faintly foreign intonation.

"She was always neurotic. I don't know why he married her." A second woman.

"Is she getting the best possible attention? I want to call in another doctor." The first woman again, agitation building in her voice. She continued: "Get the key to her apartment. We should investigate, find out what she took. We'll need her medical insurance papers. I believe she had a cat. Has somebody fed the cat?"

Sylvia didn't wake, but she continued to breathe normally. Her face turned once in my direction, following me as I crossed to the other side of the bed. It seemed her mind was alert and she knew I was in the room, and yet she was taking in my presence through a void, as if from another planet. I watched her for hours. I held her hand, smoothed her hair. Mainly, I just sat beside her bed. I believed she could hear me, feel my touch, sense movement, and that she was perfectly conscious and alert, but she simply couldn't respond. She was suspended, floating in a strange sleep. When she awoke, she would remember everything. Now and then I left the room and dozed in the hall, on a wooden bench.

For two nights and days, I sat with Sylvia or tried to sleep on the bench, afraid to leave the hospital before she woke up. I thought it was dangerous to leave her; too unlucky, too risky. I'd be out in the city, far away, doing nothing to sustain her. My presence was necessary; touch, voice, thoughts.

The Spanish doctor drew me into an office on the second morning. He said again that Sylvia would recover, but he was more sober, more judicious. He said it was a medical miracle that she was alive, but I mustn't expect too much. She'd been unconscious for a long time. No telling if she had suffered brain damage. "She might no longer be the person you remember."

I noticed, for the first time, that he was very young and had a round face and thick, curly black hair. He made an impression of physical compactness, energy, and warmth. I began to sense the qualities of his personality, his desire to be kind, and something about his idea of himself as a doctor. He was probably younger than me, but speaking in a fatherly manner, doing what he believed he should, trying to prepare me for the worst that could happen. I didn't believe Sylvia had suffered brain damage.

During the third night, as I slept on the wooden bench outside her room, I was awakened by terrible shouts in a German accent—"Seel-vya"—and the sound of hard slaps. I rose and looked into the room. The doctor who had refused to do the tracheotomy was bent over Sylvia, shouting her name and slapping her face, as if she were a very disobedient child who refused to wake up. I pitied him, but I hated him, too, and wished him ill. Sylvia didn't open her eyes.

The next morning I went downstairs and sat in the reception area. A black man and two women, perhaps his wife and his sister, stood waiting there. They were nicely dressed, as if to show respect for the hospital. The Spanish doctor appeared. As he walked toward them, his round face opened with expectation, like their faces. For an instant it seemed he was about to receive news from them. But it was he who spoke:

"Your daughter died. I am so sorry."

I then understood his expression. He'd imitated what he saw in their faces, their expectation, to show that he felt as they did. It was instinctive, a reflex of imitation, he wasn't deliberately showing anything; he was simply feeling as they did. The black gentleman said, "She only fell down the stairs." The women embraced each other and cried, and then the man cried. I felt sorry for all of them and for me.

I restrained my own tears. The thought came to me that there had been a sacrifice. A woman had died. Therefore, Sylvia would now wake up. Too bad it had to be this way, but in God's scheme of things, there is terrible justice. Sylvia and I would soon be leaving the hospital.

I thought, If I were rich, I'd give a fortune to this hospital for the many who would receive its care, and the many who would cry. I was adrift on dreams of myself as a seer and immensely generous benefactor, and though I was sure I could run a fast mile or lift great weights if necessary, I was very tired. Somebody found me wandering about the halls. I was told to go home, Sylvia would be all right. I could go home, take a shower, change my clothes. I left the hospital. It was okay to shower.

While I had wandered in the hospital and sat beside Sylvia's bed, I'd hardly noticed the days passing. Mornings were a vague brightness. Electric lights went on and it was night. I stood now in plain, cold sunlight and was surprised to see that the city hadn't ceased for a minute. Streets flourished. There was noisy traffic. People were everywhere. A taxi pulled up. I got inside. For an instant, I didn't know what to say. Where was I going? I gave the driver the address on 104th Street. We sped west. As the meter clicked off the seconds, I studied the driver's license, his name and photo, clipped to the dashboard. It shivered with jolts sent up from cobbles and holes in the frozen asphalt. Through the taxi windows, I saw steam lifting from vents in the street and the exhaust pipes of automobiles. I looked at people on the sidewalks, each of them extravagantly particular. A mustache, like a black horizontal slash, crossed out a man's mouth, forbade attention to his weak chin. A woman wearing sunglasses, furs, and heels held a little terrier on a leash. It trembled and sniffed the concrete, seeking a place to squat.

It felt good to see familiar things, but all of it was faintly colored by fear. I'd been told Sylvia would be all right. Nevertheless, I remained vigilant. I remembered the unchanging stillness of Sylvia's face, how she didn't look back at me. Then I

SYLVIA

remembered a doctor who had arrived late the second night. His name was Warsaw. He made an impression of great competence and, as if challenged personally, he showed concern to understand Sylvia's condition. He asked, "What exactly did she take?"

"She said 'Seconal.'"

"Can you find out for sure?"

From a phone booth in the lobby, I dialed Roger Lvov. I didn't want to talk to him, but I had no choice. He'd know what Sylvia took. Sylvia told me they had taken drugs together, and I remembered that he'd given her drugs in the past. His phone rang for a long time. I hung up, dialed again, let it ring for a while, then hung up and dialed once more. At last someone picked up the phone. A man said, "It's after 3 a.m., Hamilton. You're so fucking needy, so fucking tedious."

In the background, Roger said, "Give it to me." Then, speaking into the phone, in his choked, gasping voice, he said, "If you call me names, Hamilton, I won't talk to you. What do you want?"

"Sylvia overdosed. She's in the hospital."

Silence.

Then Roger said, "Yes."

"The doctor wants to know exactly what she took."

Silence.

I heard a match being struck. Roger inhaled, exhaled. "What did she tell you?"

"Seconal."

"That's right."

"Forty-seven Seconals."

"That's right."

I hung up and went to find the doctor. Then I sat beside Sylvia's bed. The conversation with Roger only confirmed what Sylvia had said, but I kept repeating the words to myself, like an obsessed detective, as if a solution to the whole mystery of life might suddenly occur to me. Seconals. That's right. Forty-seven Seconals. That's right.

When the taxi crossed West End Avenue, I saw the building we'd left three nights ago, the ambulance waiting in the street with its hysteria of flashing lights. I remembered the rush across town to the hospital.

Feeling about in my pants pocket for money to give the taxi driver, I realized I had no keys. I rang the manager's bell. She let me in and then gave me an extra set of keys. "Your wife is coming home soon, too?" I nodded, thanked her for the keys, walked upstairs.

The cat with the broken tail was gone. Someone had probably released it in the street. For a few minutes, I stood at a window and watched the street, as if I might spot the cat. I remembered standing at this window one night and hearing a sound in the sky. I'd looked up and seen geese, high above the city, in a V formation, heading north.

I went to the bedroom. When I opened a closet door to look for a bath towel, I noticed a stack of letters on a shelf and I recognized my handwriting on the face of the envelopes. They were letters I'd written to Sylvia from Michigan. Affectionate, funny letters, but I could see from the way I'd written her name and address—too big, too exuberantly scrawled—that I'd been child-like in spirit, much too happy living away from her.

In the heat and steam of the shower, eyes shut, breathing slowly, I stood like a post, and tried not to see my handwriting on those letters, tried not to think or feel. When I got out of the shower, the phone rang. It was the hospital. They told me to come back. I dressed quickly, ran out, found a taxi.

As I entered the hospital, I was stopped at the desk. There had been a phone call from my brother. A nurse told me to return the call before going to Sylvia's room. She insisted. I phoned. My brother answered. He said Sylvia had died.

The nurse waited outside the phone booth. She told me to go now to Sylvia's room, collect her things. I'd been told to come, told to go. My feet walked to her room. I didn't remember what things I was supposed to collect. I saw a clean, white, empty bed. I saw emptiness. I left the hospital with nothing, nothing at all.

After the autopsy, I went to the morgue to make an identification. The body came into view on a lift, lying on a gurney, rising from the floor. It was about ten feet away, behind a glass partition. A black woman attendant, in a white uniform, stood at the head. Both she and Sylvia were in profile and motionless, as if both were waiting for me to give a sign that this was indeed Sylvia. She was covered with a sheet from foot to neck. I spun away, as if struck by a fist, bumped into a chair, and nearly fell. The attendant didn't look in my direction, but she'd seen my response and took it as confirmation. She and Sylvia, like figures performing in a tableau, descended slowly, silently, below the floor. In another setting it might have been hard to say which of them was dead.

Funeral arrangements were made. I bought a dark suit. Services were held in a synagogue uptown, on the west side, and then came the drive to the cemetery. It was a bright, freezing day. When the coffin was lowered into the ground, my father broke and cried. His grief surprised me. It seemed inappropriate, difficult to understand. After the hospital, the morgue, and the funeral services, nothing was left in me. No one else was crying.

On the way to the cemetery, the limousine carrying one of Sylvia's aunts had raced by mine, making itself the lead car. The same happened on the way out. I had seen Sylvia's aunt about three times in the past four years. Sylvia rarely talked about her, only her husband. Sylvia liked him a great deal. He wasn't at the burial, but he'd gone to the funeral parlor with me, where he said, "I'm not going to the cemetery. I've been there too much lately."

I ate and slept at my parents' apartment. From their balcony, I looked at the city. The buildings seemed bigger in their vast indifference to me, and weirdly menacing. Street noises in the freezing air were exquisitely sharp, as if the traffic were embattled, and kids running about in Seward Park were killing one another. The roar of an airplane gashed the sky. Everything came to me as sensations, not feelings. I had no feelings that I could name. I had no human feelings.

I returned to Ann Arbor and rented an apartment, one room with a tiny kitchen and tiny bathroom. It was the converted attic of a house that sat on a hill above a graveyard, which I hadn't noticed when I decided to take the apartment. It was inexpensive and near campus. The light was good, the house was quiet. A graduate student in biochemistry lived downstairs with his wife and baby. Across the street was a girls' dormitory.

In the mornings before leaving for campus, I sat with a newspaper and cup of coffee at the kitchen table, or I'd look out over the trees and paths of the graveyard. A young woman visited a certain grave several times a week. She wore only a suit, despite the cold weather, and was always alone. For long minutes she stood facing the gravestone, head slightly bowed, arms hanging loosely at her sides. A heavy, simple sadness. My heart went out to her, as if I could easily afford to commiserate. Poor woman, I thought, and the tears would start rising.

I didn't know what I felt for myself. I believed I was doing all right, attending classes, studying for exams. It didn't seem strange to me that I'd wake up in the middle of the night feeling certain she had called my name, but I began to dread going to sleep. I was afraid I might dream. I stayed up late, reading until my eyes burned and I could no longer follow the sense of the pages. Then I'd go to sleep, and hope to fall quickly below the level of dreams into oblivion. Once I fell into the morgue, Sylvia lying there, a white sheet up to her chin. It was like the old days, the two of us in a small room, Sylvia asleep, me miserable. I started crying, pleading with her, making no concessions to reality. My need was the only reality, more real than death. Sylvia had to stop this. She had to open her eyes and sit up. She did. I hugged her and asked if she would like to go to the movies. She said yes, but could we get something to eat first? I said we could do anything she wanted, anything at all, and we went out to look for a restaurant, desperately happy.

About the Author

Leonard Michaels's previous books are *Going Places, I Would Have Saved Them If I Could,* and *The Men's Club.* He is coeditor of *West of the West: Imagining California* and the two volumes of *The State of the Language,* 1980 and 1990. His stories and essays have appeared in the *O. Henry Prize* story collections, *The Pushcart Prize* collections, *The Best American Short Stories,* and *The Best American Essays.* His books have been nominated for the National Book Award and National Book Critics Circle Award and have been included in the *New York Times Book Review* best books of the year. He has received awards from the Guggenheim Foundation, the American Academy and Institute of Arts and Letters, and other institutions. The father of three, Michaels is a professor of English at the University of California, Berkeley.